The Hollywood Sisters

star quality

The Hollywood Sisters

backstage pass

on location

caught on tape

star quality

The Hollywood Sisters

star quality

Mary Wilcox

DELACORTE PRESS

Published by Delacorte Press
an imprint of Random House Children's Books
a division of Random House, Inc.
New York

This is a work of fiction. Names, characters, places, and incidents either are the product of the author's imagination or are used fictitiously. Any resemblance to actual persons, living or dead, events, or locales is entirely coincidental.

www.randomhouse.com/teens

Educators and librarians, for a variety of teaching tools, visit us at
www.randomhouse.com/teachers

Library of Congress Cataloging-in-Publication Data
Wilcox, Mary.
Star quality / Mary Wilcox. — 1st ed.
p. cm. — (The Hollywood sisters)
Summary: Jessica Ortiz, the shy thirteen-year-old sister of a television sitcom star, has a chance to redefine herself when she starts attending a new school, but instead she must spend her time trying to prove that she is not the person who has been stealing from the other girls.
ISBN-13: 978-0-385-73527-8 (trade pbk.)
[1. Self perception—Fiction. 2. Stealing—Fiction. 3. Schools—Fiction. 4. Hollywood (Los Angeles, Calif.)—Fiction. 5. Mystery and detective stories.] I. Title.
PZ7.W64568St 2008
[Fic]—dc22
2007002752

Printed in the United States of America

10 9 8 7 6 5 4 3 2 1

First Edition

For Anna Aurelia

The New Kid Blues

Play it cool
Don't look the fool
It's day one
At a brand-new school.

I've got a plaid skirt
And a bad-luck jinx
Push open the door
See what everyone thinks.

A famous sister
Would have got me by
Everywhere but here:
Famous Family High.

The one thing I offer
For the big debut
Is just plain me
(Plus shyness, too).

Now hear all the kids say:
<u>Woo</u>
<u>Freaking</u>
<u>Hoo.</u>

In Hollywood, like everywhere, some people hide out in the background while others shine in the spotlight. One thing sets the shiners apart from the shadows: *Star Quality.*

Do you know what makes Star Quality? Want to guess?

- Good looks? *Maybe.*
- Big brains? *Not necessarily.*
- Best personality? *Probably not.*
- Flash wardrobe? Money? Great car? *Never hurts.*

When my sister burst onto the celebrity scene, I had to wonder: Why is everyone so excited about Eva? She's been living in my bedroom my whole life. What's so *Entertainment Weekly*–worthy about her now?

It took a while till I could figure it out. Eva has Star Quality. Which comes down to this: people wonder, "What will she do next?"

You can't buy it, can't fake it, can't make it—but we know when we see it on the big screen, at school, or, for the privileged few, right there in the mirror.

I have gotten a lot more attention than other women that I find incredibly beautiful. And this has happened to me ever since I was a girl, when I was flat, had no teeth, was skinny and small as I could be. I always got more attention than anyone else. If I hadn't, I would have made sure I did.

—SALMA HAYEK

scene 1

The bad boyfriend?

The rude dude that no one understands why she stays with?

It's my first day on campus—I'm cruising the grounds with two other girls for new-student orientation—and suddenly I know why the Bad News Boy doesn't get dumped as often as he should. Because the girl keeps heading back to the familiar, even though she wants to break free.

A posh Beverly Hills academy.

No one knows me here.

It's my chance to be anyone.

A whole new me could be born! Adventurer, fashionista, comedian, best bud, popular girl-about-school!

So how do I introduce myself?

"I'm Jessica. Eva Ortiz, from ABC's *Two Sisters,* is my older sister. We moved from Anaheim. I used to be superquiet, but now it's more like I watch out for shy spasms. I had one real friend back home—this guy Leo.

Who now I never hear from. So with no guys at this school, I'm not sure what will happen. At least the uniforms mean I can't fall too far off the fashion radar, right? Right?"

The two other new girls look at me with pity. Which kind of stings, since they look about eight years old.

Combined.

Holy Sisters Academy is a K–12 girls' school and I'm starting ninth grade.

"Don't worry, Jessica." The taller one puts down her Hello Kitty backpack to pat my arm.

"Está bien, amiga," says the smaller one. Who apparently doesn't speak a word of English and still looks less nervous than me.

Our guide, a senior—or, as they say here, a Year Twelve—comes over to begin the tour. I had visited once in the spring and the campus looks the same: a collection of whitewashed Spanish-style villas centered around a small central chapel ("It's busiest during exam week," jokes our guide). Orderly rows of picnic tables gleam under striped canopies on the Great Lawn. Every part of the school is shining clean. And every part is dedicated by an alumna; little plaques name-drop near the doorways, stairwells, water fountains—even the fire extinguishers: GIFT OF MS. MONEYBAGS.

In the classrooms, long wooden tables are set up. No desks. No rows. No way to sit in the back of the room or angle a chair slightly out of a teacher's view. Nowhere to hide.

The teachers we pass are a mix of men and women, with one or two almost-elderly women wearing the old-fashioned habits that most nuns have dropped.

The setting is so new—so different from the locker-slamming, linoleum-and-concrete commotion of my Anaheim school—that I'm surprised I brought the old me along. That I ran back to my old reputation like a familiar-right-down-to-his-faults bad boyfriend.

scene 2

FADE IN.

INTERIOR SHOT: LIGHT-FILLED HALLWAY. ROWS OF DARK OAK DOORS ACCENT FRESHLY PAINTED WALLS.

CUT TO: PETITE BROWN-EYED BRUNETTE TEEN. HER HAND REACHES FOR A HEAVY-HANDLED DOORKNOB.

Holy Sisters Academy has a swimming pool, a theater, a student lounge, and tennis courts, but it does lack something: a magical sorting hat to tell me who I'm going to hang out with. *Bibbiti-bobbiti! A cutesy rhyme! Will tell me where! I'll spend my time!*

HSA relies on a more traditional approach: grill the new girl.

The orientation guide drops me off at my homeroom. Six girls look me over. Their uniforms match: red, gray, and white skirts, white tops, and kneesocks. So do their expressions: curious and . . . judging?

Hmm . . . the students were a lot smilier in that HSA brochure Mom and Dad fell in love with.

A girl with intense blue eyes and a pointy nose walks right up to me. She tugs at her light brown ponytail. Then—*what's up?*—she takes my backpack from my shoulder and tosses it onto the long wooden table.

"I'm Rebecca. We're going to be friends, since my previous best friend was tragically turned into a girl-bot. It's a very sad story. You might cry."

"Rebecca, I'm standing right here." A girl with freckles and waist-length curly red hair smiles at me. "Rebecca likes to tease me about having a boyfriend."

"Don't be fooled, Jessica." Does everyone already know my name? "The Ally you see will be sucked into her phone at the merest text message from her guy."

"Rebecca, stop freaking the new girl. You're being completely . . ." A phone beeps. Ally jumps for her bag.

"She's not even ignoring me ironically!" says Rebecca as Ally whips out her cell.

Now the other girls in the room approach, led by a tall black girl. The top half of her hair is braided in snug rows all around her head, and the rest hangs loose to her shoulders. She doesn't introduce herself; she does start quizzing me about my old school. "Going to school with boys—it stunted your growth, right?"

"Um . . . I don't think so. A lot of people in my family are short."

"Your *intellectual* growth."

"Oh. No. Not that I know of." The girls look doubtful. *Ouch.* Boys mainly ignored me, but I'm not intellectually stunted enough to confess *that.*

Rebecca elbows the dark-eyed girl. "Keneesha is a certified genius—except she flunked Remedial Politeness. Keneesha, meet Jessica."

There's a flurry of other names thrown at me from Keneesha's group—and more questions about academics and "the oppression of a male-dominated school environment." Rebecca explains that HSA offers scholarships to some of the most brilliant girls in L.A.

I don't get a chance to introduce myself because Rebecca does it for me.

Badly.

"Yes, she's Eva Ortiz's sister. Jessica is an amazing actress, plus a phenomenal singer and dancer. A triple threat."

Say what, now?

I am cursed with a somewhat threatening bad-luck streak, but as for the rest of the description . . . "I'm not really like that, Rebecca."

"Everyone knows what you've got, Jessica. You're so modest!"

"No, I'm so . . . accurate." I'm okay on the dance floor, but I can barely even act interested when my sister talks about "the call of the stage," and as for my voice? Lawn mowers sound better.

"Another DQ?" Keneesha doesn't look convinced or especially intrigued. Her group turns away and jumps into conversation about their favorite reality TV show.

"It's Liver and Pancreas Week on *Real Surgery*!"

A double bill? I'll pass. Twice.

"That's Keneesha and crew. Massive brainpower, minimum contact with reality. Here's hoping they use their powers for good." Rebecca looks at my backpack. "Is that a Hello Kitty sticker?"

"One of the girls at orientation gave it to me. For good luck." I'm not sure it's working. "Keneesha called me a DQ. What's that?"

The door opens and in walks a tall, thin blonde. She's

wearing the same uniform as the rest of us, but somehow she's wearing it *better.* She throws a nod back at the two girls behind her, who rush to carry her backpack while she checks her lip gloss.

Rebecca whispers, "That's Giselle. She's a DQ."

Somehow, I had already figured that out.

scene 3

My homeroom teacher is Mrs. Hubbard. Her round, smiling face seems to match her nursery-rhyme name. She leads the class in an opening prayer, then passes out textbooks and locker locations.

I look over my class list. I'll have most of the subjects every day, on a rotating schedule. Can you guess which one I wouldn't have had at my church-and-state-separated public school?

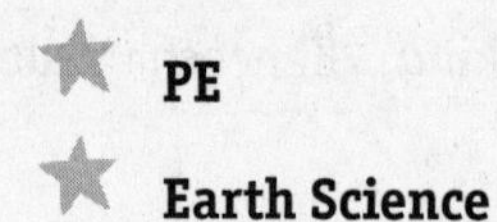

- **PE**
- **Earth Science**

- **World Cultures**
- **Theology**
- **Spanish**
- **Study Hall**
- **English**
- **Algebra I**

There's only one tough moment. When I'm asked to "say a few words" about myself. My mouth goes dry. My brain dives to the moment last spring when I stopped by HSA and mentioned that I had been "an extra in a movie." But people seemed to hear that I had been "in an X-rated movie"!

C'mon, brain! No bad-luck breakdowns!

My shyness mutates into a muffled giggle-fit, but I get out the few words required. "Jessica Ortiz. Hello. I'm happy to be here."

Okay, so the words aren't all *true.*

Not yet, anyway.

School is just a half day today—mainly picking up books and meeting teachers. There are fifteen girls in my year—and I'm the only new one.

At the end of the day, I follow Rebecca and Ally outside. The Year Nine lockers are together under a covered walkway by the Great Lawn.

I don't have much to put in my locker besides books, but the other girls seem to take locker décor seriously.

Too seriously.

I'm talking about: wrapping paper and fabric as wallpaper, photomontages, mirrors, makeup kits, and pencil holders with magnetic strips glued on the backs . . .

Rebecca is taping up cut-out pictures of bands and printouts of favorite lyrics. (Mostly from Spilt Sugar's "I Was Uncool Before Uncool Was Cool.")

Ally is putting up masses of photos of her boyfriend. She had described Dax as looking like "Josh Hartnett's cuter brother!" But you need to be wearing love goggles to see the resemblance. Ally overlaps the photos, leaving a small blank space in the center—in the shape of a heart.

She catches my eye and grins. "Lockers are kind of an HSA thing."

A girls' school where everyone has to dress alike—I guess competitiveness has to come out somehow.

I reach into my backpack. I wasn't thinking about locker decoration when I brought the photo. I was thinking of the guy whose picture I would like to plaster up on my door, leaving a too-cutesy-but-who-cares space for the heart—my sister's costar and my maybe-boyfriend: Jeremy Jones.

The picture was taken at a party at the Banks Brothers' studio over the summer. My sister and her costars are rocking the dance floor. I'm partly cut off in the corner.

Ally nods at the photo. "Fun party."

She gives me a huge pile of minimagnets and I stick up the photo. I smile when I look at it—Jeremy is pretty much the cure for a tough day.

I decide against adding the Hello Kitty sticker, which means my locker is now decorated.

Across the corridor, I notice Giselle. The DQ. Her locker door looks like a movie marquee, with battery-operated lights running along the border.

"Ally, does DQ stand for drama queen?"

Ally nods. "Figured it out, huh?" Well, I do live in L.A. With an actress. "Most of us have family who work in the business. My parents are doctors, and they only deliver celebrity babies. They're starting to think that Kiwi and Electron are normal names."

I'm curious. "What's Rebecca's connection?"

"Can you guess?"

"Studio lawyers?"

"Turned producers, exactly." Ally grins. "But the DQs don't just have showbiz connections. They are serious about becoming stars. Some have already been in commercials, TV shows, even movies."

I look back at the DQ. There is something familiar about her face. . . .

Whoa, she is sending a blaze of hate to someone right behind me. I wouldn't want to be that girl.

I sneak a peek over my shoulder.

No one is there.

scene 4

Mom, Dad, and Eva are in the kitchen when I get home. Mom and Eva are reading at the table; Dad has pieces of a small motor pulled apart on a towel on the counter. Each is trying to look like they haven't been waiting for me to walk through the door.

Eva is the only one who pulls off the self-absorbed vibe—but she is the actress in the family.

Then again, she's also the self-absorbed one. She barely looks up from her script.

"How was your day, *m'ija*?" Mom sounds casual. But she gives herself away by reaching down to give my dog—the world's most beautiful white, brown, and black English bulldog—a belly rub. And Mom never pets Petunia.

I shrug. "Not bad."

There must be more on my face than in my words because Mom lets out a big breath and swoops over for a hug. Dad nods, scoops up the motor pieces, and heads for the garage. He's whistling.

Mom picks up the phone to call Abuela in Anaheim. News flash: I survived my first day. Mom steps out onto the patio.

Only Eva seems restless.

I remember: today is her first day of not having a first day of school. Eva dropped out midway through last year when her role on *Two Sisters* expanded. She would choose on-set tutors and an acting career over high school—but you can have something you want and still want something you can't have, right?

"What are you reading, E?"

"Sides." When a movie script is confidential, the actress will be sent pages that have only her part in them instead of the whole screenplay. "I've got an audition coming up for *Malice in Wonderland*."

"Any good?"

"Argh!" Eva throws the pages on the floor and jumps on them. She's scribbled notes and character ideas in the margins. I can't tell if she's mad—or seriously into the character. "I don't know why I'm trying to give this part *depth*. It's another stupid-but-sexy monster-bait role." Eva affects a shrill mocking voice. " *'How can I defeat this creature when I'm not even smart enough to button my shirt?' "* Eva sighs. "Sometimes I think I'm making progress. Then I get sent a dozen roles exactly like my *Two Sisters* part, or else brain-challenged-babe stuff."

"I know what you mean." E raises an eyebrow. "Today my old . . . quietness came on like that horror-movie villain who won't stay dead. I beat it down all summer, but it crept back."

Eva steps over her script to squeeze my arm. "As bad as ever?"

I pause. "No."

Not as bad.

"You can't count out the fabulous Ortiz sisters, Jess. We get where we're going."

I have to wonder: since we're driving for our dreams, how can we put some giddyap in the gasoline?

When you're trying not to spend every waking moment thinking about your almost-boyfriend, it doesn't help if his face is beaming off all the channels on TV.

Jeremy has been acting since he was a baby. So

Lifetime usually has him in some child-in-jeopardy movie, HBO can be counted on to show an old disillusioned-dude-coaches-struggling-kids'-sports-team film, and Nick is constantly rerunning his previous series, *Sweetness and Sam*. The series aired five years ago, so there's a part of Jeremy that is trapped at ten years old. He played Sam opposite the cutest, chubbiest little blond girl in the world, Elle Marie. Her curls are as round as she is.

The show is starting when my phone rings. Petunia raises her head from her doggie bed when she sees me launch myself across the room.

"Hello."

"Hi, Jessica. What's up?"

"Nothing." I turn down the volume on the TV. But not in time.

"Is that the *S and S* theme song?"

New school. New girls. A talk with my sister. Playing with Petunia. It's been a full day, but nothing about the day feels as real as right now.

Talking to Jeremy.

Well, technically, lying to him.

"You think I spend all night watching you on TV? That's just the crazy talking!"

Which would be a more convincing argument if "that's just the crazy talking" wasn't the tagline for *Sweetness and Sam.*

Jeremy doesn't call me on it. "Good day at school? Everyone loved you, right?"

I want to pour out the details, but he sounds so tired. Like he can scarcely push the words through the phone line.

"Too soon to say. What about you? You sound beat."

"Yeah, *Two Sisters* all day. Then I had fight training for *Space Frontier: The Movie.*" Jeremy was cast in a *Star Wars*–wannabe movie. Principal photography doesn't start for months, but he has lots to learn—fighting, fencing, gymnastics, yodeling . . . the list goes on. He gives a huge yawn. "*Ugh.* Sorry to be so boring."

By law, minors can only be on the job for nine hours—five hours of work, three hours of school, and one hour of rest. But Jeremy's training doesn't count toward the total—and doesn't start till he gets home from his day job.

"No worries. I'll let you go." Unless you talk me out of it. Talk me out of it. . . . How tired can you be?

" 'Night, Jess. Have a good day tomorrow, okay?"

"Okay. You too. 'Night."

The click of the phone seems to be the signal that my brain was waiting for to flood with clever conversation.

Sigh.

I resist the urge to call Jeremy back, and instead download Jack Johnson's "Lullaby." I write my own lyrics to it and attach the MP3 in an e-mail to Jeremy:

When you press play, you can hear these lyrics in your head. Not in my singing voice, of course!

Jeremy once accused me of wanting to front a band. He said I had "that look." Mere moments of me assaulting music convinced him of his mistake.

Are the lyrics I write for him too much? Are they too lame? Too *girl-friendy*?

I click on Send before I can talk myself out of it.

When you've been working
All day on the set,
You're feeling bone-tired
But you're too wired to rest . . .

All the work that you do,
The people you play,
Let all that acting
Just slide away.

'Cause the best part of all
Is just you,
So I wrote this song
Just for you.

A new lullaby
All for you.

Two seconds later, it's obvious: *too girl-friendy! Way too girl-friendy!*

Two seconds too late.

scene 5

My sister and her publicist are taking the studio eco-limo (a black hybrid Lexus RX 400h with tinted windows) to the set this morning. They're going to drop me off at school on the way.

I explain how I'll be spending most of the day building my personal Web page. It's another "HSA thing"—this one all about self-expression, communication, and technology.

And . . . publicity?

"Great way to manage your message, Jessica." Keiko does a fantastic job of promoting my sister's reputation with the press. But has it skewed her view of reality?

"I don't have a message."

"Then get one! Never let others decide your image—first rule of my business." Keiko's dark eyes flash under her choppy platinum bob. "How about *Star Sister*? Or the *Curiosity Kid*?"

Which part of Keiko's slapping a tagline on me says that I won't let others decide my image? "No thanks."

"I could have the *Two Sisters* publicity team Photoshop

your picture," offers Eva. "Smooth out your skin. Highlight your hair. Add a sparkle to your eye."

A wildly offensive yet appealing offer. "No thanks." I don't want everyone to be disappointed to meet me in person.

The limo arrives at school. At Anaheim the luxury vehicle would have turned heads, but it's one in a crowd here. The stretch Hummer with the whirlpool is barely getting second looks.

"Thanks for the ride." I scramble out quickly because pep talks like theirs? Could make a cheer squad cry.

scene 6

The Year Nine through Year Twelve girls were told to go directly to the chapel this morning for a welcome from the principal.

I zone out during the great-expectations-and-good-luck speech because Rebecca is whispering to me. "Ally is a great girl. I don't want you to think she's a total melonfarmer just because she spends assembly texting Mr. Wonderful."

I'm confused. "Melonfarmer?"

Ally is on my other side. She is text-messaging her

boyfriend but looks up to say, "Rebecca collects words . . . like the ones that get patched in for curses on TV. It's weird."

Rebecca growls. "Your mother has a smooth forehead."

"That's the worst insult in Klingon," Ally explains. She doesn't look offended. Not being a *Star Trek* alien and all.

Rebecca elbows me. "I'm just saying, Ally has good traits—when she remembers she has friends besides Dax."

Conversation is cut off because the opening prayer is done and it's time for the school song. I focus on the sheet in front of me. The lyrics read:

HSA, our mother,
Lighting bright our way,
Shining precious wisdom
To guide us all our days.

I mouth along without actually making noise. Beside me, I hear Rebecca singing a different tune:

"HSA, our mother,
Has to have her way—

Just don't ask what happens
To girls who don't obey."

She winks at me. And I feel a laugh coming on. I worry that it's another nervous giggle-fit.

But it's not.

Then it's back to our lockers to pick up our books for the day.

I open my locker door.

And there it isn't.

My photo of Jeremy.

It's gone.

The magnets are all still there. Did the photo somehow slip away?

I look in my locker and on the floor. No picture. Beside me, I peek over Ally's and Rebecca's shoulders. Their photos and pictures are fine. Of course, I do have the kind of luck that would find my locker among a hundred others to make trouble.

But still.

Weird.

Scene 7

My homeroom class is gathered in the tech lab.

Keneesha and the Scholars are applying artificial-intelligence technology so that their Web pages generate automatically, based on a given matrix of information. The DQs are adding a karaoke function, complete with Pro Tools, the voice improver behind a lot of Grammy winners. Giselle's voice comes through the speakers as smooth as a milk shake and twice as sweet; ears want to stop whatever else they're doing to listen to her.

Me?

I'm trying to decide whether I should admit my real favorite movie or try for something cool-approved.

I peek over at what Ally is putting together.

ALLY

I'm not going to talk about Dax right off just because someone (Beks baby!) thinks I will. I'll only say: I

love him more than sunshine! Xxoo, Sweetie!

I also have the best friends in the world! Everyone says it, but it's true. I love you guys!

Favorite movie: When Harry Met Sally

Book: The Little Prince

TV: Seventh Heaven reruns (don't judge me!)

Motto: It's nice to be important, but it's more important to be nice.

Seventh Heaven? Not too cool-conscious. Rebecca doesn't look like she's worried about how her page will be read either. Her ponytail is bobbing as she pounds the keyboard.

REBECCA

I am a Bel-Air babysitting

mogul—made it big in the biz at the tender age of 12. Ring-a-ding-bling! Anything to keep my cat, Baffles, in premium catnip.

There's a long list of things I mostly suck at but still love to do: flamenco dancing, roller-skating, guitar, finding the perfect word.

Today's word: melonfarmer. Sample usage: "Stay away from Baffles' scratching post, you melonfarmer!"

Best physical feature: Allygator says my eyebrows. I would think she's being mean, but she's Ally, so it must be an actual compliment.

"Al, what's my motto?" She pauses.

" 'Silly String and Slinkies make anything more fun!' "

"Really?" Rebecca looks surprised. "I need a new motto."

Time to face my own screen.

JESSICA

Favorite movie: The Sound of Music

Not cool-approved, I'm guessing. Keiko wouldn't let me do it. Good thing I left her in the limo.

There's a commotion from Keneesha's area. "We're in," she announces.

"In where?"

Rebecca grins. "They hacked into the Web pages that the TMS guys are building."

"TMS?"

"From our brother school." Rebecca stares at me. "*Whoa.* You don't know anything about this place, do you?"

I didn't get a copy of *The Big Book of Everybody's Business*—which my classmates seem to have committed to memory—if that's what she's asking.

Ally explains. "The Manley School—it's the boys' school on the campus next door. We have some classes and club stuff with them, like the school newspaper." She blushes under her freckles. "Dax goes there."

Keneesha starts reading. "Listen to this guy: 'Watch for me in my Aston Martin convertible (yeah, that's how I roll).' He lists his weakness as 'chicks, man, chicks: the trick question of the universe.' "

Rebecca laughs. "He sounds hilarious!"

"Bad sign." Ally frowns. "Rebecca has such terrible taste in guys, if she likes him, you know he's got some serious deviant behavior going."

Rebecca frowns. "It hurts 'cause it's true." Then she turns to me. "Need some help, Jessica?"

"Where do we start?"

"Well, we can brag about your acting credits and vocal range later. Let's get right to the psychological stuff: which dysfunctional Care Bear do you most identify with?"

scene 8

The rest of my morning goes all right—except in World Cultures. Where I get a crash course in DQ Culture.

The teacher splits us into discussion groups. I get matched with Giselle and one of her DQ henchbabes. Who looks familiar: long blond hair, sporty.

OMG—she's my Rude Tennis Neighbor!

The girl next door who's been snubbing me since we moved in. She doesn't acknowledge that we've met before. Not that me saying hello and her ignoring me is much of a meeting. Her necklace spells out INGRID in blue diamonds.

The small-group assignment is to discuss a hypothetical foreign culture where the native people worship the "rac." They let the creature tear up their land, and spend huge quantities of wealth and natural resources serving it. Providing for the rac's needs has even led to conflicts with other countries.

Giselle looks completely bored. Ingrid cuts a glance at her, then copies her pose.

Around me the other groups are buzzing.

So I throw out: "Is it like in India, where the cow is sacred? In America, hungry people would be seeing lunch, where others are seeing—"

"No." Giselle doesn't even look up from the note she's writing.

"What?"

"No, it's not like that. Mmmkay?"

"I meant as a metaphor."

Now her eyes do rise. And pin me with scorn. "Please—this is such a 'gotcha.' We're supposed to think we're discussing some third-world nation, come up with smug 'solutions,' then feel all *ooh-aah* enlightened to find out what the rac really is."

What does she mean? I love to get to the bottom of any mystery . . . but Giselle is so rude, there's no way I'm admitting I don't know what the rac is.

"Should I *spell* it out for you?"

Spell.

That's a clue, obviously, with the way she's leaning on the pronunciation. But to what?

Giselle drags out a sigh. "Rac, r-a-c. It's backward for *car.*"

"Oooh," says Ingrid. Which she amends, with a glance at me, to "Duh."

Cars. So the exercise is about our culture. The way we pay and pave for cars—and battle for the oil to keep them going. And live in cities like L.A., where every morning it looks like it's going to rain, but it's that the sun hasn't burned off the smog yet.

The teacher calls everyone back to the circle. Then she moves to the board, ready to write down all our ideas for advising the "primitive" rac worshippers.

I steal a look at Giselle. She's not nice. But she does make me wonder: what is she going to do next?

The Nose.

Snorkel Lips.

Feet Breath.

Man Hands.

Lots of my Anaheim teachers had nicknames hung on them, but it's not such a thing here. Guys must be the ones who hand them out.

My study hall monitor is the only one whom none of the girls call by her real name. The nameplate on the desk reads: SISTER VERNA. To all of us, she's Sister Spacey.

One look at the tiny elderly nun tucked into the blue old-fashioned habit tells me why. She is tipped forward in her chair, staring at the unknown. She's earned her nickname.

The room cliques off into Scholars, DQs, and me, Ally, and Rebecca.

I'm surprised to see that the Scholars are all reading the same book: a thriller called *Hott Water*.

"I thought they'd be reading physics for fun."

Rebecca explains. "They would, but the author of the Tempest Hott books is an alumna. Raven O'Rourke donates most of the scholarship money."

Ally is smiling when she pokes my arm. "For PE next week, we've got ballroom dancing. With the TMS guys."

"Forget PE." Rebecca seems to change the subject whenever Ally brings up her boyfriend. "It's the school shows we should be thinking about. Giselle and her flying monkeys have dominated for the last year. We've got Jessica now!"

I'm not sure how the rumor that I had any acting talent started, but I have to stop it.

Soon.

As soon as I give Ally and Rebecca other reasons to like me. Until then . . . I change the subject. "So how long have you guys been friends?"

"We met in second grade."

"Rebecca grabbed my Polly Pocket tour jet and told me we were going to be friends. Her previous best friend, Fishy Fish, had been flushed to the great beyond." Ally grins. "Rebecca favors the direct approach."

"Exactly. That's why I had my brother set me up on a date."

"Rebecca! You can't force the finding-someone thing!" Rebecca seems scared to lose Ally to her boyfriend, but is she also competitive with her too?

"Shut the front door!" scoffs Rebecca. "There are lots of guys on my brother's fencing team. And with all the stuff I've got on him, he has to help me."

I can't hide my surprise. "You're *blackmailing* your brother?"

"I'm helping him do the right thing. Providing valuable moral guidance."

Ally frowns. "I don't think that's how the Dalai Lama would handle it." Rebecca is starting to look mad. "Okay, okay. Spill it. The big date. Where was it?"

"We met by the soda machine in the fencing hall. Ask me what he talked about."

"And he talked about . . . ?"

"His online community, Wizards of Enora. Insisted I call him Gandor the Good."

"No! And you . . . ?"

"Might have accidentally said Gandor the Geek."

"Did the date . . . ?"

"Go downhill from there? Rapidly."

"But he didn't . . . ?"

"Say that taking me out felt like cheating on Lady Erin-Beth? He did."

"So he . . . ?"

"Dumped me for a video game character."

Ally does not know what to say. After a moment, she comes out with: "Could have been worse."

"Lady Erin-Beth is part muskrat, part amoeba."

Ally doesn't answer. She ducks behind her geometry book. I pretend that I have to urgently tear out a piece of paper from my binder.

Which is when I notice a crumpled note.

That didn't make it into the garbage.

I pick it up, planning to throw it away.

But I'm curious.

No one is watching me—certainly not Sister Spacey, who couldn't be farther away if she jumped on a rocket.

The note reads:

Danger increasing.
Betrayal abounds—
and cuts deepest
from the ones you
trust the most.

Whose handwriting is this? Was it written for a class assignment? It doesn't sound like it. Could it have anything to do with my missing Jeremy photo?

I don't want to seem weird, rooting through old notes.

I crumple the note back up.

And tuck it in my skirt pocket.

When a guy tells me I'm cute, it's not something desirable. Cute is more like what you want your pet to be.

—NATALIE PORTMAN

scene 1

"She's the cutest little angel on earth!"

"Such a beauty!"

"Look at that smile!"

Do you want to know what it's like to be treated like a celebrity? Go help out at your grandmother's bingo game.

Such a fuss!

From the minute Mom drops me off at the St. Joseph's church auditorium, everyone wants to hug me, tell me how pretty I am, and grab a minute of my time. The compliments keep rolling in.

Even if sometimes they're a bit confused. "She's going to be a real home-wrecker!"

I'm pretty sure Mr. Singh means *heartbreaker.* I smile and nod.

Bingo is also the only place where I get asked my favorite question: "Getting taller, Jessica?"

For the past year and a half, I haven't grown an inch (or a half inch or a quarter inch or any part of an inch). So it's only when I'm dealing with people who are shrinking that comments on my height come up.

All I'm saying is: to the brilliant and discerning members of the St. Joseph's Bingo League, I've got Star Quality. That the rest of the world has somehow overlooked. As far as recharging from my first week at HSA, this trip to our old Anaheim neighborhood is a lot cheaper than a visit to the Fred Segal spa.

The players sit at foldout tables in the church auditorium, facing a small stage. There in front of the thick red curtain is a desk with a spinning jar of bingo numbers. I pluck out the number and hand it to Mrs. Sanchez, who is seated at a microphone next to me. She announces the number.

Of course, Mrs. Sanchez could easily reach into the spinning jar herself, but that would mean the bingo grannies couldn't compete over whose grandchildren help out the most. Eva and I take turns; we're in stiff competition with Mrs. Sanchez's twin granddaughters for "most devoted."

In fact, Eva was supposed to come tonight, but she

is squeezing in some more practice screams for her *Malice in Wonderland* audition. E called Abuela to cancel, but she forgot that our grandmother has a serious hearing problem.

Poor Abuela.

She can't hear anything she doesn't want to hear.

The only thing Abuela *could* hear was that I would be coming instead.

The night has its usual highlights: Mr. Singh absently calling out "bingo" every minute or so; Miss Chang claiming she can't make out the numbers on her card—as a way of flirting with Grandpa Wexley; and, most thrillingly, the moment when "B4" comes out of the jar.

I hand over the stamped white ball. Mrs. Sanchez calls out, "*B*-four!"

"And after!" the crowd calls back. I'm not entirely sure what the joke is, but it seems to get funnier every time.

After the games, over decaffeinated coffee and nondairy, nonfat, nonglucose muffins, the conversation turns to the upcoming Senior Sing-Out: the annual talent show put on by the devoted grandchildren.

THE RULES OF SENIOR SING-OUT:

- **Proud grandma or grandpa brings grandchild to the stage.**
- **Grandchild performs . . . from cutesy toddlers making up new words to old songs ("Tinkle, Tinkle, Little Star," anyone?) to high schoolers playing band instruments.**
- **There are no winners or losers in the show.**

Officially.

Officially there are no winners or losers.

Unofficially? Eva has been winning the thing since Abuela first put a plastic Mickey Mouse guitar in her arms ten years ago. And Mom, Dad, and I have been cheering her on from the front row.

"You're sending the twins for voice lessons just to compete with my Eva this year," Abuela teases Mrs. Sanchez.

Mrs. Sanchez gets a little pink around her lace collar.

"That's not true, Lucia. The girls have natural talent! It would be wrong of me *not* to encourage them."

Abuela gives me a nudge.

The competition? Doesn't scare her.

scene 2

The guy best friend.

Leo Takashi and I were next-door neighbors and best buds back in Anaheim. When I moved to Beverly Hills, I found out exactly how much geography had to do with our friendship: *every-freaking-thing.*

I called. I texted. I wrote. His silence spoke volumes. He did send me a copy of his latest zine, but other than that, not a word. Till tonight.

I'm already in bed and drifting off to sleep. I keep my cell under my pillow, for reasons that may or may not be related to Jeremy Jones. (Big phew: Jeremy texted to say he liked the lullaby I sent him.)

When the familiar number pops up on my cell screen, I can't believe it. "Leo?"

"Jessie!"

And that's all it takes. I should be mad at him for blowing me off for the past three months, but I'm too happy to hear his voice. "What's up?"

"Nothing changes here, Jess. That's why you left, right? How's Beverly Hills?"

For some reason, it's the mysteries that leap to mind . . . my lost locker photo of Jeremy, and the note about "betrayal."

I push those thoughts aside. So much has changed since I moved. Where do I begin?

I pause.

I realize that Leo and I have never had a real conversation on the phone before. Partly because we lived next door to each other; and partly because our friendship was all about activities—biking, eating, helping with homework, working on his zine, *doing* something.

Our longest "personal" conversation may have been this Hallmark moment from five months ago:

"Jessie, do you think your sister would ever go for a shorter, younger, less popular guy?"

"No."

Touching, huh?

I'm foggy with nostalgia when Leo cuts in: "The soccer club is having this car wash to raise money, and the guys all challenged each other to ask a girl . . ."

OMG!

The d-a-w-g! Dawg!

He finally calls . . . and it's to use me for a date! Could he be a worse friend?

"It's next weekend. Do you think Eva would go with me?"

Yes. Yes, he could be a worse friend.

I'm not even sorry to break the news to him. "No, Eva is flying to Boston. They're filming on location."

Leo sighs. "Thought I'd try." What am I going to say if Leo hits me up to be his backup date? I don't have to worry for long. "Guess I'll ask Lilly Schwab instead."

Eva: size skinny, hazel eyes, brown hair.

Lilly: the opposite. Lilly has cropped butter-blond hair, blue eyes, and is heavier than she wants to be.

I blurt out, "They're so different." He doesn't say anything. "Looks-wise, I mean."

"Lilly's nice, man." Leo drops his voice. I know what's coming. Some kind of secret. "She's different from Eva, but . . . it's all good."

"What?"

"You heard me."

" 'It's all good.' "

"Exactly." Is he speaking in code? Before I can ask, he says, "Too bad about Eva. You know, the two of you combined would be my perfect girl."

I hear the teasing in his voice, but I can't resist. "Yeah?"

"Eva is hot and glamorous, and you know I'm alive!" He busts up laughing.

Me? Not so much.

"Hey, Jessie." His voice drops again. "Why do you girls always go to the bathroom in packs?"

What? Is this a guy-girl information exchange? Back in Anaheim, a lot of our friendship was about ignoring that I was a girl. "I don't know. It's social? If we're always together, we know we're not missing anything."

"Ah." Another pause. Then: "Could I tell you about this dream I had?"

"Sure." Hold on! How well do I know this new Leo? "If it's not a sexy one."

"Oh. Good night, Jessie. Great talking to you."

Over and out.

scene 3

The headline blares: *"Jeremy Jones Is in Love!!!"*

My stomach plunges.

Keiko puts all the Hollywood tabloids in the limo so Eva can flip through them on her ride to the set.

The new *Tiger Beat* showcases a smiling Jeremy with the heading: *"Jeremy Jones Is in Love!!!"*

The subhead is: *"With kickboxing!"*

Freaking subhead.

Jeremy texted me this morning to say that he has another exhausting week coming up. Working on *Two Sisters* full-time and prepping for his movie nights and weekends has him beat. I don't know why he can't just "act" like he's kickboxing—isn't that what a fight choreographer is for?—but the studio is making him learn the real skills.

I toss the magazine and flip through the *Los Angeles Record* to the gossip column I love to hate, Hollywood Hype.

Scream Test

Which two TV teens, as close as sisters, are fighting for a role in a new thriller? Only one can win the part—so is it getting scary on set?

Keiko catches the headline over my shoulder. She takes the paper and folds it away without a word.

Eva gets curious. "What's that?"

I don't have to be a natural-born detective to know that one of E's costars on *Two Sisters* is competing with her for the role in *Malice in Wonderland*. Or to know that Keiko thinks the news might distract Eva.

I jump in: "E, for English tomorrow, I've got to read a poem. In front of the whole class. Any advice?"

Babies and the rattle of a key chain.

Petunia and her pink plastic squeak toy.

My sister and any talk about acting.

Some diversions *always* work.

Eva instantly forgets about the newspaper. She starts sharing her tips: "Focus on the piece! Lose yourself in the interpretation! Let your nervous energy power you through but not control you!"

I never thought of my sister as hiding behind her work. But maybe the best disguise is to disappear in plain view.

Eva asks for the poem, and I hand over the book.

I chose Emily Dickinson's "Tell all the Truth but tell it slant" because to me, the world sometimes seems like it's at a slant. Like the truth is waiting to snap into focus when I'm ready to see it—about big things like how I fit into the Beverly Hills life, or small things like my missing Jeremy photo and the "betrayal" note. Dickinson sounds like she's teasing me; like we're in on a mystery. Or a joke.

E surprises me with a dramatic reading:

"Tell all the Truth
but tell it slant—
Success in Circuit lies
Too bright for our infirm Delight
The Truth's superb surprise
As Lightning to the Children eased
With explanation kind
The Truth must dazzle gradually
Or every man be blind—"

Keiko applauds. "Fantastic! That's the heat to bring to your *Malice* audition!"

I'm not sure how "Help! The beastie stole my bikini!" can create the same heat, but I guess that's where the *acting* comes in.

"I was inspired." Eva smiles. "This poem totally relates to acting. How drama reveals a deeper truth." Yikes, put down the actress-colored glasses, E. "Would it help if I recorded the poem for you to listen to?"

"That'd be great."

"You should come to my audition this evening. Might give you some ideas for working the piece?"

"Thanks, E. You're the best."

Eva winks. Puts on her Hollywood voice. "Who's your sister, baby?"

scene 4

I've got my backpack over my shoulder and the poetry book in my hand when I make my way to the lockers. I'm trying to hold on to the glow that Eva gave me when she read.

I tap on the bookmark. It's one of Mom's: "Books make everything better."

"Not counting *Mein Kampf,* I guess," says Rebecca, tugging out the bookmark and flicking it against my arm.

My dreamy mood is broken by Rebecca's giddy one. "Sign-ups were posted for the fall musical auditions this morning. Finally, a year when Giselle's voice won't be making the local dogs howl."

"Why's that?"

"*Duh.* Jess-Jess-the-actress, you're going to win the lead role!"

Stranger things have happened.

Not that I can think of any.

I open my locker while Rebecca chatters on about my upcoming solo career.

The creepy-freakies crawl over me. But why? What's wrong?

Ally interrupts. "C'mon, you two! We've got ballroom dancing with the TMS guys!"

Rebecca rolls her eyes but hurries after her. Something feels wrong to me, but I shrug it off.

I follow them around the corner.

For a minute.

I follow Rebecca and Ally to the outdoor patio where the Year Nine girls are gathered when suddenly I know I've got to take another look at my locker.

"I left something in my locker, Ally."

"Get it later. Class is about to start."

But I can't wait.

Because what I left? I think it was my sanity.

The locker alcove is just a few steps away. I rush back around the corner and whirl through my combination.

And there on my locker door are the magnets Ally had given me. Only now they're talking magnets. They say:

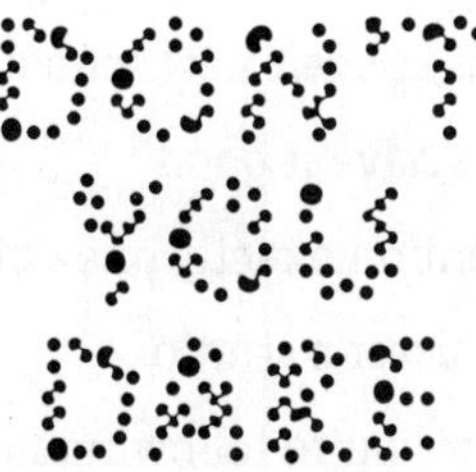

Something my life was not lacking: opinionated locker decorations.

What in the world?

Am I seeing something that's not there? Is someone warning me not to go to dance class? Has my bad-luck jinx landed me with a haunted locker? From the Great Lawn, I can hear my PE teacher calling class to order.

I scrabble my hand over the magnets, messing up the message. It's going to take more than waltzing to get my mind off this mystery.

scene 5

I'm living in a horror movie. First I've got a poltergeist in my locker. Now this: the Ghost of Bad Kissers Past.

"Jessica!" Other girls can kiss a guy, hate it, and not have him show up at their new school.

Man, other girls have it good.

"Hi, Alex." I went on exactly one date with Alex Banks; his dad owns my sister's studio.

He laughs. "Now you're following me to school!"

I'm not sure which part of desuctioning Alex from my face convinced him I was crushing on him, but the misconception lingers. Like spit on silk.

Ally and Rebecca are staring at me as if I've stepped out of a daytime drama: yes, these are the (excruciatingly awkward) days of my life.

"Ally, Rebecca—this is Alex Banks. My . . . friend."

"Sorry, Jess. We can't be more." Alex winks. "Hate the game, not the player."

He waggles an Aston Martin key chain in front of me,

then glides back to his friends—who all look impressed that he crossed the otherwise impenetrable guy-girl border. The TMS and HSA students are piled on different sides of the patio. We look like opposing preppy armies—the TMS guys are each wearing khaki pants, a black and yellow striped tie, and a white short-sleeved button-down shirt with an elaborate crest embroidered on the pocket.

Ally's boyfriend might have been the one to break ranks, but he's home sick.

"Alex is totally cute!" gushes Rebecca. Alex is short, with black hair, gray-green eyes, and an impaired sense of personal space. "Set me up, Jessica."

Yeesh. She does have wrong-guy radar. "I would. Except Gandor the Geek would start looking like Mr. Wonderful."

When the words *Mr. Wonderful* cross my lips, Rebecca's eyes cut to another TMS guy. He's sitting in a silver wheelchair, and he's definitely handsome—wavy dark hair, brown eyes—despite the stubbly patch of fuzz on his chin.

Before I can ask if Rebecca knows him, the PE teacher

announces: “We’re dancing in nature’s ballroom here on the Great Lawn patio! And we have a special treat—Will Dorsey is going to accompany the music on his violin.”

“Go, Peach Fuzz!” shouts one of the TMS guys.

Of course the others join in with a chorus of “Peach! Fuzz! Peach! Fuzz!”

The guys do love the nicknames, don’t they?

Will grins and rubs a self-conscious hand over his wannabe-goatee. A violin case is tucked beside him on the wheelchair.

The first girl to sweep onto the floor is Ingrid. Giselle isn’t in class today, so Ingrid gets to take the lead among the DQs.

The PE teacher models the steps, then matches us into pairs. I’m partnered with a supertall redhead who doesn’t say much; he’s conserving his energy for making his hands sweat.

The music gets going, and after the initial awkwardness fades, something fun starts to happen. Will blends a mellow violin tune with the music on the CD.

Only Keneesha is struggling. Partnered with Alex, she starts to look a little dizzy. He alternates too-close squeezing with speedy, spinning turns. I'm getting vertigo just watching.

I stomp my partner's foot. "Sorry." Beside us, Keneesha excuses herself to visit the nurse's office.

" 'S' okay." My partner gets a little pink under his freckles. "Do you ever go to the *Two Sisters* set?"

I'm wondering how this guy knows I'm Eva Ortiz's sister, when suddenly I realize I know his Hollywood connection: his brother was on *Survivor: Island of the Ex-Girlfriends.*

I don't know my partner's name, but somehow I overheard the *Survivor* gossip . . . must be that weird school osmosis where somehow facts become generally known.

"Do you know Paige Carey? The smartest, hottest, sweetest girl on the planet?"

I stumble again. "I know *a* Paige Carey."

My sister's costar is a gorgeous blond former model . . . who says things like: "You know the Academy Awards, right? They're like the Oscars of show business, and I totally have a fifth sense that I'm going this year!"

Following that? Like nailing Jell-O to a tree.

The music stops, and the couples separate immediately.

Overall: a little bit awkward, with the potential for fun and learning something new. A good description of waltzing class, and a possible forecast for life at my new school.

Our teacher has put out a selection of CDs on a long table. We each have to choose a few to listen to at home, then return them to the library.

The DQs grab random CDs and wander away from the patio. I get in line behind Will. Alex is in front of him and keeps offering CDs from the table. Each is well within Will's reach from his chair.

"Do you want this one?"

"I can get it, Alex." Alex drops it in his lap. "Thank you. But I can—"

Alex picks up another one. "This one?"

"I can—" *Plop*. "Thank you."

Alex's invasion of personal space has never seemed so rude. Not even when we were face wrestling! But Will is not going to the angry place. He straight-out won't allow himself to be frustrated. He's got some reserve of calm.

That I don't have.

I want to yell at Alex! Or at least watch Will roll over his foot.

Suddenly: *Thwap-thwap!* A couple of the TMS guys start throwing wadded-up balls of paper at Alex. *Thwap-thwap!*

"Real mature!" Alex bats away at the paper while Will silently rolls past him.

The whole sequence seems almost like a dance—with figures moving around the floor, negotiating for space. And respect.

That's what I'm thinking when the screaming starts.

scene 6

Ingrid is howling like a wounded animal. Has she gotten voted out of the DQ clique, or . . .

"My pictures were stolen! Someone broke into my locker!" The photomontage that decorates Ingrid's locker door does look picked over. "Me and Jennifer Aniston. Me and Dakota Fanning. Somebody took my favorite pictures!"

I see that the family photos are still up. Mom and Grandma didn't make it to the "favorite" category.

The rest of us girls from PE arrive at the same time as

Giselle. "Don't everybody look at the new girl," Giselle says loudly. Huh? Now everyone *does* turn and look at me. "I'm sure she can tell us where she was."

Ally sounds shocked. "Giselle! What are you talking about?"

I stand up straight. "I was in class with everyone else. Where were *you*?"

Giselle narrows her eyes. "I had an extra voice lesson. The other side of campus till right now."

"Ahem, Jessica?" huffs Ingrid. Who says *ahem*? Seriously. "You were late to class. Way after everyone else was there."

"What? That's because I thought someone broke into *my* locker." Why does my voice sound so breathless? "Um . . . you know, my picture was stolen too. Last week."

Giselle's voice drips skepticism. "And you're mentioning it *now*? How convenient."

Rebecca jumps in. "Back off, Giselle. That's just the crazy talking."

Giselle scowls. She spins away. "It's time for Spanish, *muchachas. Vámonos.*"

Ingrid makes a big show about staring at me and playing with the lock on her locker before she stomps off. "I'm reporting this to the principal after class."

Ay, yi, yi!

scene 7

The scene with Giselle leaves me shaken all through my morning classes. I can't even concentrate enough to stress about reading my poem aloud tomorrow.

Ally, Rebecca, and I are having lunch on the quad under one of the striped tents before I remind myself to get out of my head. It's an old shyness trap—forgetting to be in the moment, ignoring the real conversation around me.

Wait, that's what I'm doing now! *Concentrate!*

". . . and that's why Dax's mom named her kids after her character's husbands on *Days of Our Lives,*" Ally explains seriously.

Okay, this time I didn't miss much.

Ally gets a text from her guy, who is home fighting a fever. Rebecca sighs. Ally's eyes won't be off her cell for the rest of the period. "Ally, try not to be jealous of my fabulous new friendship with Jessica. She's not going to drop her friends for some guy."

Well, not *some* guy. Maybe one guy . . .

Then I get to hear about Rebecca's latest adventure in dating. How does the girl find time to do any homework?

Then again, these "dates" don't seem to last beyond splitting a Coke after fencing practice.

"So we met by the soda machine after practice. Scott wants to be an actor."

"Was he interesting?"

"Too interesting. He kept trying out these different personalities. It was like speed dating, but with one person."

"Do you think—?"

"We'll go out again? Well, I'd go out with the funny guy from the first five minutes, and the laid-back sports guy from the last two minutes, but I don't ever want to see the weepy, angry-at-Mom guy from the middle four minutes again."

Even though Jeremy's texts to me for the last few days have been brief—"thanks for the song" and "must sleep now"—he's starting to seem like the greatest potential boyfriend of our times. At least compared to the members of a certain fencing team.

Rebecca smirks. "Of course, it won't be easy to tell the last guy apart from the other two. They all—"

"Dress alike?"

"Exactly."

I'm almost smiling when I catch a glare from Ingrid at the DQ table.

Rebecca pulls at her ponytail. "Jess, I didn't see your name on the tryout list for the school musical."

"About that . . ."

"So I signed you up. It's *Annie Get Your Gun*!"

Erk.

It's going to be *Annie Get Your Earmuffs* if I'm singing.

I can't put off this confession any longer. "Rebecca, I can't sing."

"You're so modest! That means self-effacing or diffident."

"Um . . . yeah, I knew that one." I take a deep breath. "Full disclosure? I cannot sing. The grandmas at bingo turn down their hearing aids when I hum."

"What?" Rebecca looks genuinely puzzled. "But you mentioned you were in a movie. And I know somebody told somebody that you . . ."

"*I'm* telling you that I'm not." Reminder: not all those stories that float around are true. And how did my being an extra in one of my sister's movies turn into an all-star résumé?

A few stanzas of the school song would convince Rebecca I'm telling the truth.

But the full truth? I like her too much to do it.

scene 8

Auditioning means putting on your best face, trying to fit the part while a roomful of strangers coldly looks you over.

It's like the first day at a new school!

Every time!

No. Thank. You.

For the *Malice in Wonderland* audition, Keiko and I sit on metal chairs in a large room with Eva. Mom is waiting outside in the car. Her audition jitters can be contagious.

I love being in my own clothes: hot pink T, jeans, and gold Chinese sandals. Slipping off the HSA uniform felt like slipping off the day's problems.

The audition room is bare except for chairs, a poster from the movie *Horror High*, and a camera set up in the back for taping the performance. Three large windows face the parking lot. Eva has seated herself so that she is backlit by the center window; the view from the doorway creates a natural frame around her. E has that visual sense of what first impression she wants to create. I've got my own spot—anywhere that doesn't cast a shadow on E.

Keiko runs through final points. "Do you want to go over the core mission of the film?"

Eva pulls an insincere smile. "Giving the viewing audience a big high five for being idiots?"

Keiko manages to laugh. Barely. "It's not Shakespeare, or even Spielberg, but you do have this one big scene. They're going to be looking for real passion. Even tears."

Eva nods. "Got it."

Keiko pats her bag. "Do you need anything to help get to the right emotional space?"

"What?"

"I brought eyedrops, menthol, tissues with bits of chopped onion in them—to help with the crying."

"Not necessary." Eva looks at me. "When I need to cry, I think of something horrible happening to Jessica."

My head jerks up. "What?"

"It's a *compliment,*" insists E.

Keiko reaches into her bag. "Okay, but the tear stick is here if you want it." The tear stick looks like a white lipstick in a clear case. Keiko uncaps it and the smell of menthol almost makes *my* eyes water. "Dab a bit under your eyes, and the burning will get the tears going."

Yowch!

The casting director and director of the film enter. Both women are cheerful and professional. They give Eva the rundown. As usual, Keiko had the inside track: they are looking for an emotional connection to the character.

"I'll give a three-two-one lead-in," says the director. "Then I'll cue you. Okay?"

E nods.

The director faces the camera. "Eva Ortiz. *Malice in*

Wonderland reading. Three, two, one . . ." She points to E.

Before Eva opens her mouth to speak, I get a nervous jolt.

I start fiddling with a metal joint on the side of my chair.

Something is wrong.

Something about Eva is . . . what's the word? Cold.

EVA

Why? Why did this have to happen to Chester Cat?

CASTING DIRECTOR

He was in the wrong place at the wrong time with the wrong killer mutant jabberwocky.

EVA

Was anything left of him?

CASTING DIRECTOR

Just his teeth.

EVA
(Boo-hoo!)

Eva squeezes out some tears—what is she imagining is happening to me?—but something about the reading was flat.

I tug at my chair leg anxiously.

Eva and the casting director do a second read together. This time I can make out the individual steps of E prepping to cry: stiffening the muscles in her eyes, opening them wider, not blinking.

There usually isn't much feedback at an audition—the director wants to keep all her options open. But the pause after E's performance feels especially empty.

At last the director says, "What would be your character's reaction if Chester Cat showed up later? He isn't dead after all—just missing a set of false teeth?"

An improvisation.

She is kicking Eva a challenge to test the depth of her connection with the character.

Eva responds: "My character would be happy."

Whoa. Could she have phoned that in any worse? Only if she was talking into a tin can on a string.

Keiko, E, and I say goodbye and exit the room. I can almost hear the audition reel hitting the garbage can as we leave.

Weirdness.

E has a natural ability to find the right note with a character and then refine and repeat it. Maybe she wasn't "on" today?

We're walking out through the lobby when, with a flash of her camera-ready smile, Eva's energy ramps up from sleepy to showtime.

A familiar voice calls out: "Eva!"

Paige Carey, *Two Sisters* costar and (I guess) *Malice* contender, and her agent are waiting. "How'd your audition go?"

"Mega-amazing!" Keiko is always *on*. "Couldn't you hear the sobbing out here?" She would completely tear stick herself if it would help Eva's career.

"Did you know that they cast Rachel McAdams as the lead? I'd love to work with her!" Paige pauses. "Or just have her be jealous of me." Then she starts quizzing Eva:

"Who was in the room? How's the space set up? Did they throw any surprises at you?"

Eva grins big, then gives a few answers and air kisses for good luck.

Paige sighs. "You'll probably get the part. You're so lucky."

"I am?"

"Sure. The camera subtracts ten pounds from you."

"Oh. Um. Thanks."

"Plus you make really brave choices. And I'm not just talking about the way you dress."

Eva pauses. Squeezes out a "Thank you."

Hmm . . . can you imagine if Paige was *trying* to be insulting?

"Anyway, it doesn't even matter who gets the part. We're all winners." Paige flicks a look my way, stopping short of adding: *Not you, Jessica.*

When we finally exit, E has not mentioned the surprise question. She whispers to me: "It wouldn't really be improv if I'd warned Paige, right?"

Actresses usually keep quiet on audition details, but

I'm surprised E is so competitive about a part she doesn't even want.

Eva checks her watch as we get into the car. Mom glances at Eva and then doesn't say a thing. She reaches over to squeeze her shoulder.

"Can we hurry?" asks E. "I'm going to be late for bingo."

"What? *That's* what was on your mind?" Keiko never criticizes my sister. But she does sound horrified.

Eva shrugs. "I promised my *abuela*."

I don't have to be Jessica Ortiz, Girl Detective to see the deeper truth. Yes, my sister loves our *abuela*. But she does not love *Malice in Wonderland*. Even an actress can't always force a connection.

I have a sudden urge to tell that to Rebecca and the Boys' Bel-Air Fencing Club.

I try not to have expectations and just be open to possibilities.

—ROSARIO DAWSON

scene 1

The limo is rolling along this morning, and so is my stomach.

I printed out my Emily Dickinson poem. I read and reread it. My iPod is on a loop, playing Eva's recording of it.

For a distraction, I peek over Keiko's shoulder at this morning's Hollywood Hype.

Break a Leg

Wedding Crashers star Rachel McAdams turned into a furniture crasher when a chair leg collapsed under her at a *Malice in Wonderland* audition. The actress was not injured, but she does hope to keep further cracking up confined to her comedy hits!

What? Is it possible that Rachel sat in the chair I was pulling at during the audition? I would say the chances aren't that great . . . except for my jinx.

Eva shakes my arm to get my attention. She packs the trip with suggestions on "connecting with the audience" and "interpreting the artistic vision of the poet." She doesn't seem bothered that she didn't connect or interpret at the audition yesterday.

My brain buzzes. Concentrate. Review the poem. *Be* the poem. And if I feel like I'm going to pass out . . . aim for something soft.

I stumble through my morning classes with my mind tossing and tumbling the lines. When it's finally time for English, I realize that I left the printout of the poem in my locker! You don't have to be Freud to see that slip.

I hurry back to my locker—and can't find the poem. Can't find it. *Can't find it!* Where is it?

I tear my locker apart.

No printout.

Did someone steal it? Was it my poltergeist? My bad-luck jinx? Or could it be my . . . poem that's peeking from my skirt pocket?

Check.

I clutch the printout and race down the hall. I'm able to slide in late because the lights are out in the room. Keneesha's poetry reading is accompanied by an audio-visual PowerPoint presentation projected onto the white-board. The only bright spot in the room.

Keneesha shares a collection of poems that were created for the Epitaph Project. Experimental artist Joyce Burstein purchased a plot at Hollywood Forever, a cemetery next to Paramount Studios. On the headstone, she put up a chalkboard, then invited passersby to write their epitaphs. Keneesha's PowerPoint shows people writing on the stone, and close-ups of their inscriptions. She reflects on the power of language as we struggle with mortality, ending with her own epitaph: "To Be an Achiever, Be a Believer!"

The girl is a full-on genius: she figured out a way to give her reading in the dark! With all eyes focused away from her!

When the Scholars are done applauding, Keneesha excuses herself. She promised to share the presentation with the Hollywood Forever trustee committee.

Rebecca doesn't wait for the door to close behind Keneesha before she stands up and gives an intense reading of Hilaire Belloc's "The Microbe"—a detailed description of a creature no one has ever seen, ending with " 'Oh! let us never, never doubt/What nobody is sure about!' "

Was she thinking of my actress/singer reputation when she picked that?

Next Ally gives a reading. She speaks too quickly and softly but brings sincerity to the main line: " 'Life is short and we have never too much time for gladdening the hearts of those who are traveling the dark journey with us. Oh be swift to love, make haste to be kind.' "

And then, as they say in the circus, the moment we've all been waiting for.

Giselle takes the stage. It's just a cleared-out space in the front of the classroom, but she *takes* it. Makes it her own. The class watches while she expertly applies a false mustache and goatee. Checks her look in a hand mirror. And launches into a falling-down-funny rendition of part of Byron's "Don Juan."

She brings perfect comic timing to the transition of Juan's speeches from lovesick to *seasick*:

"'Oh, Julia!
—(this curst vessel pitches so)—
Belovéd Julia,
hear me still beseeching!'
(Here he grew inarticulate
with retching.)
. . .
No doubt he would have been
much more pathetic,
But the sea acted as a
strong emetic.'"

" 'Emetic,' " whispers Rebecca. "From the Greek, meaning something that causes vomiting."

The way Giselle is rolling around on the teacher's desk, the meaning is pretty obvious.

Everyone is laughing. Except for Ally: "That's mean. A sick boyfriend? Not funny."

Giselle takes her bows from atop the teacher's desk.

"Were you doing Will Dorsey's voice for Don Juan?" Ingrid calls out. "You sounded like him."

"Please. I haven't seen Peach Fuzz since last year." Giselle tugs off the fake goatee. "That was vintage Johnny Depp."

And then . . . the moment no one has been waiting for.

I trudge to the front of the class. A dozen pairs of eyes eat at me.

Then, apparently, I make a decision: I'm out of here.

scene 2

"I can't believe you did that, Jessica!" Rebecca is in awe. We're having lunch on the Great Lawn. "You were amazing!"

She's right: I was amazing. And I should know—I watched the whole thing.

Here's what happened in English class:

I approached the podium, ink from the printout staining my sweaty palm. I stopped to give my teacher the poem to check against my reading.

And then,

I floated

. . . up!

. . . up!

. . . up!

And out of my body!

I don't know how else to describe it.

I looked down at "Jessica" reading the Emily Dickinson poem. My eyes were on myself, and I was giving the best reading imaginable. I completely channeled my sister. Eva's voice—her emphasis, her energy—came out of my body. When the last words left my lips, I floated back into myself and took a seat.

You could have heard a . . . fingernail crack. Giselle rapped her hand too hard on the desk.

Even now, there's a part of me that's still dreaming . . . drifting . . .

Diving to the earth in a blazing fireball!

Crash!

☆

"Give them back, Ortiz."

Giselle and the DQs surround my side of the lunch table.

"Give what back?"

Giselle leans over, her bony arms folded. At this closeness, the soft breeze reveals the tops of her extensions. "My photos. The ones you stole from my locker."

"What? I never took anything from you."

"I saw you sneak into class late. And now my photos with Tyra Banks and Rachel Bilson are gone. So give them back, klepto."

"Giselle!" squeaks Ally, at the same moment that Rebecca jumps to her feet.

"Those photos are worth money!" shouts Ingrid. "And everyone was there for the whole class except for you . . . and Keneesha."

A sudden hush.

At the next table over, almost as one, the Scholars put down their Tempest Hott books.

There's an awful pause.

Giselle looks like the scene has gone wildly off-script. "Just give 'em back." She rides off in a cloud of Christian Dior's Poison, with her posse following.

And me?

I'm not floating. I'm sunk, slouched, slumped into my body. Lumped somewhere in my shoes.

scene 3

Keiko and Eva pick me up after school. Since Keiko manages reputations for a living, I want her advice.

The trick? I can't reveal exactly what I'm up against.

Keiko thinks I'm a disaster magnet. She once banned me from the Banks Brothers studio because of the way celebrities and freak accidents tend to intersect when I'm around. I just had to sit in a chair for it to endanger Rachel McAdams! (Well, sit and pull at the leg screws.)

"Jessica! It's great that you want to know more about being a publicist. Remember, if you're going to announce controversial news, wait till late Friday and hope everyone forgets about it over the weekend. If you're really on the hook, wait for a major holiday weekend."

My questioning may have been too subtle.

The way things are going, I don't think I'll make it till Thanksgiving at HSA. Or even till Friday.

"And, of course, call in the star power in times of emergency. Like how the *Two Sisters* costars went to Paige's fashion show after her battle with bad press."

I look at E.

And I don't have to ask.

"Why don't you forget to bring your lunch tomorrow?" suggests Eva. "Then I can drop it by."

Eating with Eva under the awestruck eyes of the HSA girls? My PB&J will be tasting sweet.

Goodbye, Beverly Hills. Hello, Anaheim. It's my evening to help out at bingo.

But does the sea of print dresses, drugstore perfume, and wallet photos provide a getaway from controversy?

Not tonight.

The St. Joseph's Bingo League Senior Sing-Out: *this time it's personal*. Eva's domination of the event in past years has brought some competition.

Mrs. Sanchez has been busted for hiring a personal stylist for her twin granddaughters. Grandpa Wexley was visiting his son (not the Doctor, the Other One) at the Corner Café when Mrs. Sanchez exited the Star Stylin' Boutique next door. She confessed to the professional prepping under interrogation with a side of crumb cake.

Abuela only says: "Mrs. Sanchez must do what she must do."

Oh yeah.

That's grandma-speak for "Bring it, baby!"

Abuela is not worried. Not a bit.

Which reminds me: I haven't seen Eva practicing her act. . . .

scene 4

I get to my locker early this morning—but not early enough.

"Unfunny, Ortiz." Ingrid is waiting for me. She slams a green Post-it on my locker door. "This creepy note was stuck to my Spanish book. I don't know what you're doing, but quit it."

"Me? I'm not doing anything."

I can't help staring at the note.

What makes you afraid?
Loss. Of possessions, friends,
family . . . of self.
Reinforced by time—the

time to wonder . . . what is coming next?

"Ingrid, that's not even my handwriting. It's old-fashioned and swirly."

Her muscled tennis arms flex as she clenches her fists. "Don't try your mind games with me!"

Logic is a mind game?

I hadn't heard Rebecca arrive, but she suddenly jumps in with a blistering insult. If you're a Klingon.

Ingrid looks more confused than enraged. "Of course my mother has a smooth forehead. She goes to the best Botox guy in L.A."

With that Ingrid crumples the note and throws it into the trash can. A perfect shot.

"Remember what I said, Ortiz. Just because the principal said there's no evidence for her to go after you doesn't mean I won't." She gives me a nasty, body-tracing look. "This ends now."

As soon as she's rounded the corner, I turn to Rebecca. "Whoa. What does Ingrid's family do? Write for soap operas?"

"They're special-effects coordinators. Mostly explosions."

"Oh."

Well, that doesn't scare me. Much.

Taking a deep breath, I head to the trash can. I pluck out the note.

Rebecca watches. "Jessica? Anything you want to tell me?"

What can I say? That I'm a wrongly accused locker thief on the trail of a threatening note writer?

Rebecca would have to share her favorite expression: That's just the crazy talking.

Every time Rebecca says it, I want to mention that it was a tagline on Jeremy's show. My almost-boyfriend Jeremy Jones. But I'm not sure that Rebecca could handle another friend with a boyfriend—almost or not.

So I'm betting all my marbles that Eva's appearance at lunch today will wash every worry away.

"Nothing to talk about, Rebecca. Thanks."

She stares as I open my backpack and put the "fear"

Post-it in an envelope. Right next to the "betrayal" Post-it I'd found before.

For once, Rebecca doesn't say a word.

scene 5

All morning I see Year Nine DQs taking down favorite pictures from their lockers. They glance at me, then tuck the photos into their handbags or folders. Is it a vote of confidence that Ally and Rebecca leave all their photos up?

The hours drag until I'm seated under the striped canopy on the Great Lawn. Waiting for a delivery of lunch . . . and star power.

Ally is texting her guy. Rebecca is talking about her upcoming birthday party. All the Year Nine students at HSA and TMS are invited.

Not Rebecca's choice. Her parents'.

L.A. is a one-business town, and Rebecca's producer parents are always thinking about their next movie. The kid in Rebecca's theology class could be the godchild of the next superstar, agent, or Crafts Services manager they want to work with.

For the same reason, most parents will make their kids go, whether they like Rebecca or not.

Before I can check out photos of the party location (Moonlight Rollerway Skating Rink), I hear the three words I've been waiting for. "Lunch is served."

But Eva's voice has never sounded so deep.

Or barrel-chested.

Or male.

I squeeze my eyes shut and mutter, "When I open my eyes, I'd better see my devoted, would-never-let-me-down sister standing here."

"You got it, Jessica!" I creak an eye open. At my dad. "Well, every part but the sister."

Instead of Eva Ortiz, star of screen and stage, may I present Robert Ortiz, star of oil change and reliable engine repair?

Ooh. La. La.

"Rebecca, Ally—my dad."

"Eva got called in for script reworking, and I was

home." E sent me a text message this morning, but I've been afraid to open it. Dad nods at Rebecca and Ally.

"Thanks, Dad." I test our father-daughter psychic connection, sending him a blast of mental energy: *Leave, Dad. Please, say nothing embarrassing and go.*

He sits down next to me. "All rich kids at this school, or what?"

Our psychic hotline? Not so hot.

Instead of answering his question, I set Dad up for a show-your-coolness conversation. "Dad, tell us about the time you rescued that baby from a runaway car."

"There was a runaway car." He pauses. "I took the baby out of it." As the master of the modern American story, Toni Morrison is not sweating the competition from my father.

Ally nods seriously. "Very brave, sir."

Rebecca agrees. "Audacious, gallant, and downright spunky."

"Not really. It was over before I even thought about it." He shrugs, then smiles. "I'm glad to see you have friends, Jessica."

My face heats up. "Um, Dad . . . why wouldn't I . . . ?"

He turns to Ally and Rebecca. "Jessica can be a bit shy, but she has a lot going on. A *lot*."

And then my dad proceeds to "sell" me to my friends.

His heart is in the right place. But I still wish the rest of him was anyplace but here.

Dad beams. "And has she shown you her poetry? She's great."

While he brags on, I stare at my lunch—and suddenly I do feel a poetic spark.

That I do not share.

In ketchup, I spell out
"Save me" on my plate.
A cruel universe
Ignores my fate.

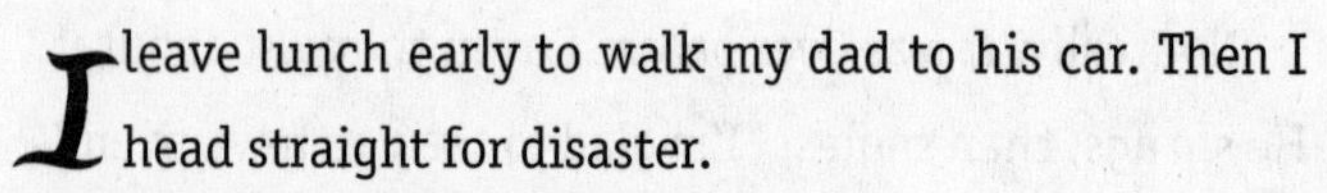

I leave lunch early to walk my dad to his car. Then I head straight for disaster.

I mean, straight for the lockers.

No, wait. I was right the first time.

"My science fair championship photo!"

"My pictures from physicists' camp!"

"My Mathletes team collage!"

That's right. The Scholars' pictures have been stolen.

Then I hear:

"Baffles!"

"My heart montage!"

Rebecca and Ally were hit too.

Ally hides her face behind her long curls. Rebecca stares openmouthed.

Rebecca's exact expression is hard to read.

To me it looks depressingly like I've been downgraded: from "potential friend" to "What Ortiz girl? We've never seen a shy brown-eyed girl with a famous sister around here . . . and she had weird hair, too."

The worst part? I have the bad feeling that I haven't even hit bottom.

Yet.

Scene 6

I'm too distracted to squeeze a juicy apology out of Eva for standing me up at lunchtime. Which is too bad, since I would have fully enjoyed access to her new Chanel lace-up boots.

Instead, almost as soon as I get in the limo, I launch into the story of my friend "Jennifer." Poor Jennifer is struggling to fit in with her new "book club." Somehow she has made enemies. What can she do to work her way out of trouble?

"I'd advise your friend to lay low at a top-quality spa through Christmas—then come raging back on the scene with a hot new music video! Or perhaps she could rescue refugees in a war-torn nation and sell the photos exclusively to *People*."

"Thank you, Keiko."

As far as helpful comments, I'm filing that under: "*N.*" For "Not."

E says lightly, "You know, I'm shooting on location in

Boston, starting tomorrow. Mom is coming. Maybe you could join us?"

Keiko's advice does come down to strategic retreat.

I'm not running away, but if something gets stolen while I'm not at school, I'll be off the suspect list.

The only thing between me and three thousand miles of alibi (and the chance to see Jeremy again!): my mom.

"Okay."

"What?"

"I said okay. Let me talk to your dad. If he agrees, I'll go online and get another plane ticket."

"What?" I had prepared a long alphabetical poem of reasons to convince Mom to let me join the trip to Boston.

And yes, it does sound best if read to the beat of Maria von Trapp's "Do-Re-Mi" song.

"A, a land, a land I love.
B, the birthplace of our nation.
C, I must C it for myself!
D, Don't leave me at the station!"

That's where Mom stopped me. Abruptly.

To say that I could go.

At first I thought my poem had worn her down (I didn't say I'd written a *good* alphabetical poem). But it was something else that convinced her.

"*M'ija*, this motherhood thing? Ever since you girls were past the "don't eat that bug" stage, I've been going on instinct."

"What does that mean?"

She brushes back my hair. "My instinct says let's take this trip together. You, me, Eva."

I'm thrilled! And insulted!

Exactly how pathetic do I look?

Then Mom names her price. "You haven't wanted to talk about your new school much. But we'll have time for a good sit-down on this trip, right?"

I've told my mom some things about school: homework, meeting Ally and Rebecca, being embarrassed to ask for a bathroom pass when at HSA, if you have to go, you just . . . go. But Mom knows I haven't told her everything. Maybe it's living in Hollywood, but I'm still hoping to have a happy ending before I fill her in.

While Mom talks Boston with Dad, I take Petunia for a walk. I stop right at the edge of my Rude Tennis Neighbor's driveway. I could march up there and talk everything out with Ingrid. Convince her I'm not the locker thief. Then we'd get all the Year Nine girls to work together to figure out what's happening.

I look at my feet.

They're not moving.

Sometimes my feet are smarter than my brain.

scene 7

In our Anaheim life, Mom might have taken E and me on a surprise trip to In-N-Out Burger in the Nissan—now we take a jet to the East Coast. And it's first-class all the way. Even the city tour that Keiko set up for Mom and me is private.

Look closely.

Can you spot the big difference between Boston and

L.A. in this sentence?: I'm walking the Freedom Trail with my mom.

No, it's not the presence of the Bunker Hill Monument, the Paul Revere House, and the Old South Meeting House (where colonists dressed like "Indians" before launching the Boston Tea Party). It's the *walking*.

Los Angeles is a motor city. Even when I toured the Warner Bros. lot, I rode a trolley. And, of course, all the celebrity homes sightseeing tours are conducted on buses. Here it's *walk-walk-walk*.

Everyone!

Children, old people, and women wearing Jimmy Choo slingbacks!

Mom and I are in the Old North Church, sweating through a freak heat wave. We're listening to a fake colonist in a real tricornered hat read from Longfellow's "The Midnight Ride of Paul Revere":

"He said to his friend,
'If the British march
By land or sea from
the town to-night,

Hang a lantern aloft
in the belfry arch
Of the North Church
tower as a signal light,—
One if by land, and two if by sea . . .'"

The guide points out the ways that Longfellow got the story wrong—the British would have come by river, not sea (going by sea would have taken them in the wrong direction); and the lanterns weren't to signal Paul Revere, they were for the American militia.

Eva would find the actor's work insufficiently enunciated, and lacking a certain Orlando Bloomish ability to carry off the knickers and kneesocks. But he gets me thinking.

I came to Boston to get perspective on the mysteries at HSA, and this story gets my brain buzzing. . . .

The "friend" in Longfellow's poem was Robert Newman, sexton of Old North Church. He slipped out his bedroom window and into the church. Then he climbed the steeple, hand over hand up the rungs. He flashed two lanterns briefly. Unluckily, the colonists were not the only ones to see the lanterns—British troops also saw them. They broke down the door of the church—with Newman escaping out through a back window just in time.

But not really.

Through the process of elimination, the British reasoned that only the sexton would have had access to the church at that hour. They arrested Newman.

Process of elimination.

I mentally review the clues to the HSA mystery: the threatening Post-it notes, the photos stolen from the lockers, the magnets spelling out "DON'T YOU DARE". . . . I can't see a motive that would hold everything together, but maybe I can get close to the truth by ruling out the suspects.

The boys of TMS are not on campus enough to be the culprits, and the Scholars all have alibis for at least one of the trespasses, even Keneesha, since the last robbery was during lunch. Giselle claimed she was at a voice lesson when Ingrid's photos were stolen—which might not be true, but she was at lunch for the last thefts. Wasn't she?

I guess anyone could have slipped out. I was too busy talking to Rebecca to notice.

Now, if I eliminate the suspects who have likely alibis, the person with the best opportunity to cause all the trouble is: me.

Freaking process of elimination.

Beside me on the church bench, Mom says, "That's a serious face." I shrug. Mom is on leave from her library—but that doesn't mean she's forgotten how to dig for information. "Anything you want to talk about?"

"I told you about my classes. And my homework." I put on my listening face like I can't be distracted from Fake Paul wrapping up his story.

"Please note the collection box at the back of the church. It's original to the church, dated 1723, and believe it or not, it still works today!"

Ha. Ha.

Boston even has old jokes!

scene 8

At the gift shop of the posh—and mercifully air-conditioned—Copley Square Hotel, people are doing their best to pretend not to notice my sister. It's still odd to me that people get excited to witness Eva buying a pack of gum—elbowing each other, or snapping the not-so-secret camera phone picture. *Oooh,* the over-the-shoulder shot . . . that dude must have had Special Ops training.

The shop's book rack is selling the latest Raven O'Rourke novel, *Hott Water*. Tempest Hott has inside information that a flood is coming, but she can't get anyone to believe her. From the cover art, it looks like she hijacks a ferry to rescue zoo animals. There's no author photo to check out the HSA alum, but you know she's a former DQ type, don't you?

The book gets me thinking about school, and I drop Ally a quick text. She texts me right back—with lots of information about Dax's cold (the girl seems dangerously close to collecting his old Kleenex as souvenirs)—and says that Mrs. Hubbard gave a speech about respecting personal property and working together to stop the thefts. Nothing suspicious has happened since I've been away.

Ah. What a relief.

I sure don't want anything bad to happen at school.

I'm close to 100% sure that I don't wish ill on my school for the selfish reason of my having a perfect alibi. Because that's the kind of almost-good person I am.

☆

And shallow.

I'm an almost-good and shallow person.

I don't mean to be, but there it is.

Boston offers the country's oldest college (Harvard), library (Boston Public Library), and major-league baseball stadium (Fenway Park)—but my favorite sight? Not so historical.

Only fifteen years old, in fact.

Jeremy Jones is wearing jeans, a white V-neck T-shirt, and a smile. A tired smile, but it's all for me. We run across a crowded field of wildflowers into each other's arms. Magic!

Ish.

Magic*ish*.

Technically?

Technically, it's a wildflowerless crowded lobby, and Jeremy gives me this weird half hug, half back pat. But still: Magic! Ish!

Then he is whisked away. The moment I'd been waiting for . . . turns out to be *literally* a moment.

He barely had a chance to whisper: "My schedule is packed, but I'll call if I get free, okay?"

"Okay." I plaster a fake smile across my lips.

Then he's gone.

Now a "Jeremy Jones mystery" might be bothering you. *Does the guy really like Jessica when he can't find any time for her?*

Yikes! That's not the mystery I was referring to. That's the one I keep buried in the back of the brain.

I will not admit that I'm in denial.

The *other* Jeremy mystery: why haven't I mentioned him at school? Why haven't I played on my almost-girlfriend status for popularity points?

Answer: because it's more important that Jeremy sees

me as cool-at-school girl than that my school realizes, *Jeremy Jones likes you! So now we do too!*

At least, it's more important until another crime gets pointed my way and my popularity really plunges.

Which I'm starting to think is exactly what's going to happen next.

scene 9

Another day in Boston, another text from Ally saying "all is well" at HSA.

Is that a clue?

What if nothing is going to be stolen while I'm away because *the point of the stealing is to pin it on me*?

Bizarre. But possible.

Normally, I would need an Eva-sized ego to think that so much effort would be directed my way, except that:

- Mine was the first photo to be stolen.

- The magnet message was written on my locker—and no one else's.
- The thefts seem to be timed for when I'm the most likely culprit.

And what about the threatening notes? Was I meant to find the "betrayal" note? Did Ingrid give me the other note . . . as a warning?

These clues might mean I'm the real target of the locker trouble, or as I'm now thinking of it: Project Photo Frame-Up.

I don't mean to sound like I've been snoozing behind the wheel of the Mystery Machine (I'd have to forfeit all Scooby Snacks), but when your sister is a star, you get used to all the attention going her way. If my hair was on fire, I'd still expect the first glass of water at a restaurant to go to E.

Now, like my colonial forebears, I realize that a new world order is required to meet these changing times.

Yes. It's true. I'm giving in to Mom's talk-to-me eyes . . . and asking for her advice.

Eventually.

Eventually, I'm asking my mom for advice.

Currently, I'm listening to her latest lament about the challenges of raising teen daughters. This rant is directed, surprisingly, at the free, low-budget newspaper *Shopping Time*.

"Look! Look at what they are selling."

I flip through and see pages of winter boots, coats, and snowmobiles. "Don't worry, Mom. We'll be back in L.A. before the cold weather."

"Jessica, I mean look at what they are not selling. Our local *Shopping Time* is packed with plastic surgery ads! And I didn't even notice that until I saw this one." Mom frowns. Boston is giving her a new perspective too. "What else are you girls exposed to without my realizing?"

"Mom, please. You know that E and I would never go under the knife."

She looks relieved. "Not even to pin back your ears?"

"No." And thank you. Mom has been spending time in the tact-deprivation chamber again.

"*Gracias a Dios.*" She lets out a long breath. "Now, what did you come in here to talk to me about, *m'ija*?"

Not my ridiculous clown ears, if that's her guess.

I glide around the subject. Which is: how do I invite Jeremy to Rebecca's birthday party to help me fight back on the popularity front?

But I don't glide gently enough.

"Jessica, a cute boyfriend can't solve your problems."

It's like Mom never even went to high school! "But listen . . ."

"You have to find your own happiness, then find someone to share it with." Did moms talk like this before Oprah? "I'm glad your sister set up that educational trip for the two of you. I wouldn't want you to waste your trip pining over a boy."

First: pining over Jeremy? Not a waste.

Second: what trip?

scene 10

"Bye, Mom!" Eva gives me a secretive grin as we step out of the Copley and into the shimmery heat of the afternoon.

At first I think E is grinning because the "educational trip" she's set up is the Boston Movie Mile tour.

We get a cab—Bostonians say that everything in their city is "ten minutes away." But they are otherwise honest.

We meet the guide at the top of Boston Common, where *The Departed* was filmed. Then E herself becomes part of the tour, happily smiling for autographs and photos.

This being Boston, it's another walking tour; so why is Eva decked out in strappy, high-heeled Manolo Blahniks? And come to think of it, I don't think I've ever seen that old-fashioned white blouse and long skirt before. . . .

She is up to something.

I don't have to wait long for the first clue. The tour takes us into Beacon Hill, where posh brick row houses rise over cobblestone streets. On Charles Street, amid the fancy shops and cafés, Eva nudges me.

"Jessica, look! Don't you love his work?"

We're passing a costumed redcoat soldier in front of Ye Olde Seafoode House. He's handing out flyers for the lobster special.

"His work?"

"Yes, period acting. So authentic."

E is admiring the costumed flyer boy? If that's not a clue, then I don't have Papa Aldo's stick-out ears.

Which, we all know, I do.

I'm not surprised when E waves off our tour guide and we step out of the heat of the day and into the Beacon Hill Chocolates shop.

My sister asks for some of the gold-topped honey truffles and dark chocolate dusted with chili. The candy can't be for E; it makes her break out.

I don't have long to wonder who she is sweetening up.

Eva puts the overflowing box of treats into my arms. "Jess, Mom thinks we ran off so I could get the real scoop on your school. She thinks you're holding back."

"Well, actually, she's ri—"

"But really I'm the one who needs your help! You're the only one on my side!"

Why do I have a bad feeling about this?

Because I know my sister.

☆

"Eva, your agent wouldn't keep scripts from you. She works for you."

"She works for my 'interests.' " We're back to walking along Charles Street. Eva is pounding on her RAZR to get directions. "She thinks a corsets-and-carriages movie isn't for me."

Eva's agent hasn't been sending her scripts for any period pieces, so E was thrilled to find out that the director of the next Jane Austen film is in town finishing up his movie *Harvard Square.*

"So you have an audition?"

"Not so much an audition as an address."

My bad feeling? It gets worse. "You're crashing the set?"

"Not me." Eva smiles. "Us!"

scene 11

I thought we'd be taking the T to Cambridge, but Eva explains: All those movies about Harvard University? Not shot there. The school has a policy against for-profit filming in its buildings.

"Even *Legally Blonde*?"

"That was mostly filmed in Southern California. USC, UCLA." E stops and points at a large stone building. "The Boston Athenaeum. That usually stands in for the Harvard library."

Trailers line the narrow street—makeup, wardrobe, and one with the name *R. Witherspoon* taped to the window.

There is a security guard stationed outside the door.

"I'm Eva Ortiz. I'm in the movie." Eva likes to explore the gray area between acting and lying.

The guard is an older man in a black uniform. He checks the call sheet. "You're not on the list."

"Could you check again?" Megawatt smile from E.

Then—because it's Eva's luck, not mine—another guard steps outside. "Eva Ortiz! I'm a huge *Two Sisters* fan."

Of course he is.

Just like that, she's in.

E needed me as a cover to get away from Mom, but now she suddenly thinks it's awkward to crash the set with her sister. She tries to drop me off downstairs in some vending-machine room.

Lesson of the day: my sister does not lack for nerve!

No way am I agreeing to being left behind . . . so she runs off before I can say a word. She inherited our *abuela*'s "hearing problem."

The room has nothing in it except machines for energy bars and bottled water. Cool, refreshing water—just the thing for killer truffle-mouth—for one dollar.

Which is one dollar that I don't have. I have the "emergency twenty" that Mom makes me carry, but the machine does not give change. It only gives aggravation.

Sweating, thirsty, trapped with a bad-attitude drinks machine. Stuck in the basement of a library *with nothing to read*. At least the afternoon can't get worse, right?

scene 12

Wrong-wrong!

The ring on my cell makes this sound: *Wrong-wrong!*

That's what it sounds like to me when I check the caller ID: Jeremy Jones.

I was wrong-wrong when I thought the afternoon could not plummet straight through bad into terrible.

"Jess! We wrapped early on the 'Kitty Litterbug' scene and I've got the next hour free!" *Of course you do*. "Come join me at Fenway Park. The studio has this awesome skybox, and everybody from the show is here watching the Red Sox." *Maybe I could take a cab to the game and Eva could meet me there?* "Even your mom is here!" *Or maybe I should stay here, sweating and bored, thinking up appropriate payback for my sister? Something that involves lots of heat and little water. Or possibly lots of water and little indoor plumbing.*

"Jeremy, I'm sorry. I can't come." Mom would take one

look at me and wonder where Eva is. And no way would she approve of E crashing a movie set to try to score an audition.

"The suite is huge. Everybody is invited." In the background I can hear cheering.

"That's not it."

"Is it your bad-luck thing? 'Cause there aren't any celebrities for you to jinx up."

"It's not that." And geez! Harp on my Dumbo ears next, why don't you?

"What's up?" He sounds disappointed.

"I—I can't say."

"Are you all right?"

No. "Yes, I'm fine. If I can get there in the next hour, I will. Promise."

"Sure." Now he sounds farther away than Fenway. "Bye, Jessica."

"Bye"—*Click!*—"Jeremy."

Eva had better land this audition.

And get the part.

And win an Oscar for it.

And thank me in her speech.

And chew off the nameplate with her name and scratch in mine.

What I'm trying to say is:

The Girl Owes Me.

Big-time.

Scene 13

An Olympic athlete pounding around the track.

My dad reaching for the last churro on the plate.

An actress going after a part.

There are some situations that call up superhuman levels of determination. Ones where even the abandonment of a younger sister for *sixty-two minutes* in a small, hot room in a private Boston library can occur.

I smack my hand against the drinks machine.

"Thirsty?"

"Desperate." I turn around. I thought that voice sounded familiar. Reese Witherspoon is exactly as blond, wide-blue-eyed, and petite as you'd expect. And she gives me a dollar for water!

She's a mom, you know.

I barely cough out a "Thank you" before glugging down the drink. Then when Reese puts in her money, the machine blinks: OUT OF STOCK.

"Would you like the rest of mine?" One last swallow is left at the bottom.

"No thank you." She wipes her forehead. "Craft Services will arrive soon, I'm sure."

E is tense but excited as we enter our suite at the Copley. I'm furious but silent.

Normally, Mom would clue into the vibe, but not tonight. "My first game from the skybox, not the bleachers! If only your dad could have been there. I had to go through two rounds of security, but suddenly, after the packed stadium . . . *whoosh* . . . open skybox space. Even the air felt expensive."

Tell me more—*if you enjoy torturing your youngest, and supposedly beloved, daughter!*

"The stadium is so small that the seats practically put us *in* the game. And the suite! *Ay!* Air-conditioned, flat-screen TV, waitstaff offering fruit, sweets, and cold drinks by the bucket—all free. The studio must have bought out Boston!"

Or at least a certain sweaty corner of Beacon Hill.

"There were outdoor rows, but it was too hot. And besides, inside felt like this fun private party."

Mom picks up her cell to share her joy with Dad. I give E the angry eyes.

She is unmoved. "Is that your mad face, Jessica? Because you should narrow your eyes more, and maybe tighten your jaw muscles."

One sister for sale.

Cheap.

Scene 12

We haven't even left the first-class lounge at Logan Airport, and it's already been a long trip home.

My sister, trying to make up for yesterday, is pouring attention on me. I ignore her, but she launches into her version of the B*ah*ston accent anyway.

"It's basically a broad *A* and a dropped *R*—with the *R* then added to words that end in *A*. Like: Jehemy went to Fenway Pahk without Jessicker."

Pahk the cah in Hahvad Yahd! That's the example everyone uses! Why improvise?

Eva must notice my angry face (eyes *firmly* narrowed) because she makes the sorry-shrug and hands over her *Los Angeles Times*.

Today's Hollywood Hype? Does not make me feel better.

Too Hot to Handle

Reese Witherspoon was treated for dehydration on the set of her new Boston-based film yesterday. The city's freak heat wave, combined with an incompetent Crafts Services team, left the hardworking actress with a thirst for more than success. Hype asks: Water you thinking, Beantown?

What?

Did I keep critical refreshment from the lovely and generous Reese?

My buzzing thoughts are interrupted by a beep from my cell. Ally and Rebecca confirm via text that nothing has been stolen from school today, either.

It's clear: Project Photo Frame-Up is going to the next level. Los Angeles is my town, and I'm not going to be chased out of it.

I'm bringing a little revolution home from Boston.

As well as a tasteful get-well card for Ms. Witherspoon.

If I make a fool of myself, who cares? I'm not frightened by anyone's perception of me.

—ANGELINA JOLIE

scene 1

Back in L.A.! The land of the wannabe famous, the almost famous, and the it's-so-wrong-that-they're-so-famous.

It's even the land of the sister-to-the-famous. And the person who wants to pin photo thefts on her.

I had all weekend to wonder: why did Eva raiding the *Harvard Square* set feel like a clue to what has been happening at HSA? The dots are there. How can I connect them?

My time is freed up for mystery solving now that Jeremy is too busy to call me. (Except for the hours that I spend wondering if he really is too busy or if he's just mad that I blew him off at Fenway Park.)

"How's everything at school? Did that World Cultures quiz go okay?" Dad is driving me to school today; E has the day off.

"Fine."

Tucked in the sun visor above his seat, I see the

postcard I sent him. Including my poem called "How to Fit in when Visiting Boston."

To not look the tourist,
Follow steps one, two, three.
Don't call it Beantown.
Or wear a Harvard T.
And if a broad accent
Leaves you mistaken,
Just shout "Go, Sox!"—
And no offense will be taken.

I pull down the postcard to use as a bookmark, but Dad stops me. "Hey! I collect your poems."

I'm flattered—until he pops the postcard into the crammed glove box. Some treasure chest!

☆

Keiko's "strategic retreat" plan worked. A little. People have had a chance to think about something besides the thefts since I've been gone.

I run around all morning handing in three days' worth

of assignments. My mom will let me miss some classes "to study at the school of life" . . . as long as grades at my real school don't suffer.

Then I catch up with all my friends. And by "all," I mean "both."

In study hall, Sister Spacey is zoned out, per usual. Rebecca, Ally, and I huddle at one corner of the large table.

I like that Rebecca jumps in with a question about Boston words—instead of the "what did Eva say/do/wear" quiz most people throw at me. "Was everyone saying things like 'wicked awesome'?"

I have to confess. "I didn't hear real Bostonians talk like that."

Rebecca frowns—and I feel like I forgot to bring her a souvenir. There were some creative words for New York Yankees players—but I can't repeat them. Then something occurs to me. "They have this expression. 'It's ten minutes away.' Apparently, it's a joke to play on people to get them to trudge halfway across the city in a heat wave."

Rebecca tries it out. " 'That's so ten minutes away.' Interesting."

Ally is excited to share her news. Her freckles are almost dancing as she says her boyfriend is feeling better. She's hoping he can come to Rebecca's birthday party tonight. "Are you bringing anyone, Jess? The invites are a plus-one, you know, and the Moonlight Rollerway—could be romantic."

I duck my head. "Not sure. Maybe." There's a chance that Jeremy could be free. And a slightly smaller chance that he's still speaking to me. "What about you, Rebecca?"

She frowns. "No couples skate for me."

Ally twirls a strand of hair around a finger. "But you love skating, right? I mean, your mom wanted to host that hike through La Jolla Valley again, and you insisted on the rink."

"Yeah."

I'm afraid to ask, but . . . "No fencing guy?"

"You did miss some Coke machine dates while you were in Boston, Jess. The highlight? One of the guys paid for my Sprite. Lowlight? He demanded his money back!" Rebecca blows her bangs off her face. "Which part of 'tell me five words that mean versatile' is bad dating protocol?"

Um . . . every part?

I tread gently. "Rebecca . . . do you give *quizzes* on your dates?"

"So? They're not spelling tests." Rebecca bristles as Ally and I stare. "Anymore."

Ally asks: "But who could pass a test like that?"

That's when it hits me. *Someone* could. Rebecca's mystery someone. "Are these tests based on a guy you know?"

"What?" Rebecca looks surprised. That I caught her. "Is it so much to ask that the dude not be a total troglodyte?"

Knowing Rebecca is so going to help with my verbal SATs.

She takes off out the door. Sister Spacey doesn't even blink from the spot on the ceiling she's studying.

Scene 2

When Rebecca doesn't come back after five minutes, Ally and I split up to go look for her. Ally goes to the bathroom; I head to the lockers.

The halls are eerily empty; I pass one older guy on the cleaning staff. There isn't anyone to question me when I push outside to the locker alcove. At my Anaheim school I would have been asked for a hall pass about ten times by now. Is it because HSA charges big-bucks tuition that they assume the kids are staying in the classes?

No Rebecca outside . . . but what's that peeking through the vent on my locker? It's glossy and straight-edged like a . . . *uh-oh.*

I spin the combination on my locker and pull open the door.

What do I find? Trouble.

A pile of it.

The stolen photos stare up at me: Ingrid's and Giselle's celebrity pics, the Scholars' achievement photos, Ally's shots of her boyfriend, and Rebecca's of Baffles the cat.

What should I do? What can I do?

I check my watch. The bell to change classes is going to ring in less than one minute.

I start jamming the photos into my backpack.

Then, over the sound of my heart pounding, I hear a gasp. I look up.

"Rebecca!"

"Jessica!"

I don't know which one of us is more surprised. She puts a hand to her mouth, horrified. And runs off.

She doesn't let me explain.

That's when it hits me. As much fun as Ally and Rebecca and I have had together these past couple of weeks, I'm still the new girl. There's one thing that builds trust. The one thing I don't have: time.

The bell rings.

scene 3

Rows of book-heavy dark oak shelves fill the HSA library. Each bears a discreet plaque; I'm hiding behind the "Gift of Tahj Balmer" stacks. I'm not sure that Ms. Balmer was thinking "top-secret hideout" when she made her donation, but it works for me.

There was no way I was going to be able to choke down a sandwich under the lunch tents—and under the suspicious eyes of Rebecca. And the unknown eyes of my enemy.

I was meant to open my locker in front of all the Year Nine girls and get caught with the stolen photos. The timing of the thefts, the magnet threat, the creepy notes . . . I can't deny that they've all been directed at me.

But why?

And by whom?

And how is the person getting into all the lockers?

I didn't even know anyone here when I started, and my photo of Jeremy was stolen on the second day!

Which reminds me . . . Quietly, I open my backpack and peer inside. I poke through the photos without removing them. No sign of the Jeremy photo. Was every photo returned except mine?

I hear the librarians moving closer and duck farther back among the bookcases. The library has a huge crime fiction section. I'm not surprised to note the plaque: GIFT OF RAVEN O'ROURKE. She generously sent plenty of her own books. In *Hott Fashion,* Tempest has to rescue a clothing designer from jealous rivals. In *Hott Sand,* she leads a lost group out of the Nevada desert. In *Hott Summer,* she rescues a beached whale.

The stories sound familiar somehow . . . but I know my brain is trying to distract me from the big scary thing I must do now: text Jeremy.

I pull out my cell.

Could u come 2
a party at the
Moonlight
Rollerway in
Glendale? 2nite
@ 7. Would love
to see u! ☺

I add the smiley face icon because the sweaty, desperate face icon? Lacks the attractive.

If I could get Jeremy to show up at the Moonlight, my problems would not go away—but people would be more likely to see my side of things.

Then: a square of yellow catches my eye.

It can't be.

It is.

Another note! Who could have known I'd be here? Even *I* didn't know I'd be here!

Sin's rainbow stretches
against a soul-white
sky——from palest
gray to the black that
consumes.

When you think it can't get worse, then comes the darkest crime.

The murder of an innocent, the destruction of a soul.

I breathe deeply, dragging oxygen to my brain.

Project Photo Frame-Up just got much more serious.

Deadly serious.

scene 4

I avoid Rebecca and Ally for the rest of the afternoon.

Back at home, I get E's help in picking out an outfit for the Moonlight. And by "get her help," I mean "get caught removing her new Marc Jacobs top from her closet."

"Hey!"

"Oh, hi, Eva." I'm sorry to burn my you-dumped-me-in-the-Athenaeum-basement card in exchange for one night out with a shirt (didn't it seem worth more like all-out access to her car when she gets one?)—but . . . caught is caught.

I explain to E about the party. With a reminder about the Athenaeum, she's ready to share.

"Jessica, something vintage would work better for the Moonlight. The place is a total time warp." She pulls out a 1960s blouse by Pucci. The fabric is smooth but clingy, and the print is a psychedelic red, white, and black swirl.

No way am I leaving the house in that.

But I try it on to please E, and look in the mirror. "Not groovy, baby."

"Pucci clothes are joyful, and you forgot the most important accessory."

"Earrings?"

"A smile."

I turn back to face my sister, and then I do smile. "You are seriously starting to sound like Mom."

"Shut it, Jessica."

"It's spooky. Do you feel the need to order your wardrobe by the Dewey decimal system?"

Eva whirls me back toward the mirror. And I can't tease her anymore. She's right—a smile does pull the whole thing together.

E helps me with my hair and makeup.

"Sparkle blush? Are you sure?"

"Feel the sixties funk, Jess. Work with the disco ball."

"Oh, behave!"

I'm now fully glamorous enough to play with my dog for twenty minutes. All while thinking of what to say to Jeremy.

I pick up my cell.

It's not till I hear him answer that I realize I forgot to turn down *Sweetness and Sam*.

"Jeremy?"

"Hey, Jessica. Got *S and S* on?" His voice sounds scratchy and hoarse over the line.

"Yes." I don't even have the heart to lie to him so he doesn't realize I'm a dork! Is the magic dying? "Did you get my text about roller-skating tonight?"

"I'd like to go, but I'm feeling worn out. There's some kind of fever going around."

"Oh. No problem. It's just a friend's party—girls from my school, some guys from TMS."

"Next time, definitely. I'm so tired and hot. My throat is on fire—whenever I swallow, it feels like I'm gulping nails." He pauses. "There are *guys* going?"

"You should rest your voice."

"But . . ."

He's too nice to be the first one to hang up, even when talking hurts. So I do it for him.

But I'm still going to the rink tonight. The photo framer is not keeping me away from a friend's birthday. Tonight, I've got one more card to play. And one more call to make.

scene 5

Dad drives me to the rink. (Mom lost the privilege when she giggled about "Jessica's boy-girl party!") He reaches over to push open the door of the Maxima. "Have fun, Jess."

As far as requests go, that's an ambitious one.

I'm entering my first HSA party, where most of the girls think I'm a thief, and my friend and hostess believes she caught me with the evidence.

I'm ratcheting the "fun" expectation down to "survive the night." Fingers crossed.

☆

For the past fifty years, the Moonlight Rollerway in Glendale has been the go-to spot for skating. Mirrored balls dangle from the ceiling, and the old-fashioned electric sign on the wall blinks: ALL SKATE.

There is a Hammond organ tucked into a gazebo above the rink, and the organist is pounding out a rocking "Chattanooga Choo Choo." The DQs and some of the TMS guys are skating around the rink.

Will Dorsey rolls by me, joking that he brought his own wheels. I head to the rental counter to trade in my shoes for skates. Then I find a spot on one of the parklike wood-and-iron benches to tie them up.

I'm seated next to Keneesha and her friends.

Their interest in the party? Purely anthropological.

"Watch Giselle toss her hair. It's a signal of interest in her skating partner."

The others note signs like "dilated pupils" and "mirroring body language."

Yeesh. Way to make a party feel like a pop quiz.

I skate over to the snack bar and find Rebecca with her mother.

"Hey, birthday girl."

Rebecca looks a little surprised to see me, but plays it off as she introduces me. Rebecca is a total minimom; they share the same pointy nose, blue eyes, light brown hair, and intense vibe.

Her mom is already onto my show business connection. "I'm setting up a new film, *Hollywood Homecoming*. Tons of cameos. Might be a role for your sister. Oh . . . there's Will!"

Her mom waves and hurries off.

"Will Dorsey?"

"My parents did their last movie with his dad. That's where I first met Will." Rebecca raises an eyebrow. "You know his dad is Max Action, right?"

"What?" Suddenly it's clear where Will gets his good looks—from one of the top stuntmen-turned-action-heroes in the movies. Is Will growing that goatee to look less like his dad?

Rebecca almost laughs out loud. "Would his last name have to be 'Action' to clue you in?"

"Ease up, Rebecca." Her tone has bite. Is it because of what happened at my locker today? Or something about Will?

"I wasn't sure you'd come, Jessica."

Me either. I lower my voice. "I don't know what you think you saw, but I'm not the photo thief." I don't ask her not to tell anyone about seeing me with the evidence. There's no point in saying that. A person will either talk or not.

"Ally bailed."

"What? Why?"

"Dax said he was tired, so she went over to take care of him."

For the first time tonight, I'm glad I came. Ally is super-nice, but does the boyfriend need to come before everything?

I pull the tiny packet from my pocket. "I know you said no presents, but . . ."

Rebecca eyes the thin silver chain with markings on it.

"It's your name in Mayan hieroglyphics." I was on location with Eva in Mexico last summer and got interested in the history. "The ancient Maya thought written words were sacred gifts from the gods. The peasants weren't taught to read because they weren't worthy to interact with the higher powers."

"Thanks, Jessica." Rebecca smiles big. Then goes still. I don't know why till I hear a voice.

"Happy birthday, Rebecca."

"Hi, Will."

"Nice party. Going to take a spin around the floor?"

"With you?" Her face gets pink and hopeful.

"Um . . . actually, I'm going to get something to eat. But I'll see you out there, okay?"

"Okay."

I suspect I know why Rebecca moved her party from hiking La Jolla Valley to the Moonlight. Would Will Dorsey pass Rebecca's dating/vocabulary test?

I'm tempted to follow him, when there's a sudden hush. The blue-eyed blond costar of *Two Sisters* has made a surprise appearance.

Jeremy Jones is here!

My heart is beating like a hummingbird's; the blood rushes to my face. Jeremy crosses the rink. He's wearing a gray V-neck T and khakis. If he looks movie-star handsome, it's because, well, he is.

The crowd quiets, then parts all around him.

Ha! Try and steal this! I want to shout to my mystery enemy. *This moment is mine!*

As he moves through the DQ crowd, the rink music changes to "My Boyfriend's Back." It's the moment right before he spots me, and all I can think is: can life get any sweeter?

Jeremy speaks. His voice is raw—with his cold? Or with emotion? His words carry as every ear strains to catch them: "Is that you? Elle Marie?"

Giselle steps forward, melting against him like butter on hot toast.

All I can think is: yes.

Yes, life could get a lot sweeter than this.

scene 6

Let me go on the record as saying: spying on your almost-boyfriend and the girl who (no one but me is surprised to find out . . .) is his former costar is wrong.

Off the record?

Could you keep it down, please? I'm hidden behind the rental lockers and it's hard to hear.

"Elle, I can't believe you're here! How long has it been?"

"*Sweetness and Sam* got canceled five years, three months, and two days ago, so . . . a long time."

"You look great. If you hadn't waved at me, I don't think I would have even recognized you."

"Yeah—no more beeping before I back up."

Elle Marie had not really been as large as a wide-turn vehicle. Almost, but not quite; it was part of her sassy-style charm. The eyes are the same, but everything else is different. Who knew Elle Marie had cheekbones? Or a neck?

"What do you mean?"

Giselle sighs. "I know it wasn't you—it was 'Sam'—but your character was always ragging on my weight."

"Those were jokes! About Sweetness!"

"We wore the same pants size."

"Elle, I'm sorry."

"Not your fault. Anyway, I grew up. Lost the weight, and"—bitter laugh—"the sweetness, too. I got a reputation for being difficult. I don't know how."

There's a mystery I *could* solve.

"Hey, you're a pro. The real thing."

"Please. Most of us can't transition to teen roles. I was back slumming on basic cable! I did a season on this idiotic *Safecrackers* show, then my dad threw me into school. *Real* school—the bell rings to change classes."

"That's retro." I can hear the grin in Jeremy's voice. "Are you still singing?"

"Sure. Lead in the school shows, all locked up." Her voice drops. "Probably." Then she has the nerve to sound concerned about Jeremy. "Are you all right? You don't look well."

The girl sounds sincerely, deeply, makes-me-want-to-throw-one-of-those-disco-balls-at-her *thoughtful.*

Freaking thoughtful.

Freaking thoughtful!

FREAKING THOUGHTFUL!

Okay, I'm back. From the crazy place.

"Yeah, my throat is dry . . ."

That's my exit cue. After all, I don't want to miss my big scene with Jeremy Jones.

scene 7

I'm standing beside the rink, where Jeremy can spot me when he leaves the rental area. And I hear: "Jessie, you look amazing!" Huge hug from the guy, drawing attention from every HSA/TMS student at Rebecca's party.

The problem?

Right lines, wrong guy.

"Leo! Thanks for coming." OMG! I had forgotten that I had invited Leo to the rink when Jeremy said he couldn't come. I'm a worse drop-friends-for-the-guy offender than Ally!

"It sounded like a case for the Anaheim Avenger!"

"Um . . . okay." Can I promise Eva as a future prom date if Leo can stop referring to himself as his zine alter ego?

And what's with his new look? Leo has the coloring of his Japanese dad and the bone structure of his Dutch mom—but tonight, no one is looking at his face. His hair is gelled straight up into a fauxhawk. You have to be the coolest living dude in Hollywood (see: Maddox Jolie-Pitt) to carry that off!

"It's good to see you, Jessie. And looking a lot happier than when that moving truck pulled away."

"Three months can be a long time."

Leo shrugs. "I'm not Mr. Correspondence, but you tell me to show up . . . and here I am."

I grin. Same Leo enthusiasm. He's always in the moment. "C'mon, I'll show you where to trade in your shoes for skates."

"I'm going to hit the bathroom first, okay?"

"I'll be here."

I'm still standing beside the rink where Jeremy can spot me. And, unfortunately, where Alex Banks can get snarky as he skates by.

"Where'd your boyfriend get his hair done, Jessica? At an electrical outlet?"

Excuse me? No one wearing an all-white Gucci jumpsuit and blinged-out dog tags is in a position to insult Leo. Not that I'd engage in a battle of wits with an unarmed person.

Anyway, I have no time to waste on Alex.

Here comes Jeremy.

"Hi, Jessica."

"You came." I show off my grasp of the obvious. How impressive.

"Yeah." He coughs. "I was feeling better. For a minute."

"Oh." I cannot push another word off my tongue. Not one.

"Jess? Could I ask you a favor?"

I nod. "Anything."

"Could you look out for Elle Marie? She's an old friend, and I can tell when she's worried about something."

Anything but that. I can't quite meet his eye. "Sure. Absolutely."

I glance over Jeremy's shoulder and see Giselle watching us. She's wearing a tight black T-shirt with THE HOT DOES NOT STOP written across it, a short, swishy orange skirt, and the angry face that I seem to inspire. Yeah, I'll bring by some kibble for that friendly little kitten.

I step toward Jeremy.

Don't worry! You know I'm not about public displays of affection!

But wouldn't a quick kiss clear up which girl he came to see?

Um . . . assuming that was me.

I'm trying to casually arrange my lips somewhere in the general area under his. Then he coughs and moves back. "Sorry. Bad cold."

He doesn't want me to get sick.

Why am I doomed to like such a considerate guy? Is there no goodness in this life?

I feel a sudden creeping chill.

No, wait, that's an arm!

On my shoulder!

Ack! Leo! After all our years of churros, bike rides, and flashlight tag—*this* is how you repay me? He has flung an arm around my shoulder.

Jeremy's eyebrows go up. Way up.

"Jeremy Jones! Awesome to meet you!" OMG—Leo is *showing off* for Jeremy! He squeezes my shoulder and tilts his head toward mine.

My face is so hot that my hair is starting to singe. I knew once Jeremy and Leo were in the same room, I was dealing with a potential minefield, but this . . . "Jeremy, this is Leo Takashi. My . . . my . . ." *Worse brain cramp ever!* ". . . cousin."

"Your cousin?"

Couldn't Leo be from the Japanese-Dutch part of the family that I've never mentioned before?

I look to Leo for help. He repeats: "Jeremy Jones! Awesome to meet you!"

Okay, now *that's* the worst brain cramp ever.

"Leo." Jeremy looks like he expects me to say something. But what? He coughs again. "I better go. Good night, Jessica."

He walks off without a backward glance.

About that minefield? I think I just heard a big, bad boom!

scene 8

I'm choking on disappointment. Not because of how the scene looked to other people—like Jeremy had come to see Giselle and then stopped to say "hey" to his costar's sister—but because of how it looked to Jeremy.

Like I was with Leo. Jeremy didn't seem like he believed the cousin thing.

I let my hair swing over my face.

I'm so used to being around new people that I forget: Leo knows me. He knows when I'm upset.

"What can I do?" he asks.

"You're here, Leo. Thanks." A big part of friendship? Showing up. "Now stop touching me."

"Sorry." He whips his hand off my shoulder. I think we might have a weird moment, but Leo is just Leo. "Let's eat!"

At the snack bar, the conversation around us is all about Jeremy.

"He's so hot!" He did look hot—feverish, actually. What was he doing here?

Even Keneesha is gushing. "I got punch out of the bowl right after him."

"It's like your cup was right where his cup had just been."

"Like your cups were kissing!"

"It's like I kissed Jeremy Jones!" This girl is probably a future Supreme Court justice, but right now the logic function in her brain has been completely disabled.

I want to say: *dipping punch is not the same as kissing Jeremy Jones! Believe me!*

But no one would.

Ingrid skates over. "Quite a look, Jessica." She eyes my swirly shirt up and down. "Quite. A. Look."

I can't dredge up the smile I need to wear Pucci well. But my growl seems to shoo her away.

Leo and I eat—I had forgotten how much food he can pack away—then join Rebecca on the skating floor. He tries to charm her with his after-dinner conversation.

"Whew! I feel like an anaconda that swallowed an entire cow."

Rebecca? Not so charmed.

"What? What?" Leo calls after her. Then to me: "Do you think she likes me?"

The rink is closing, and I'm helping Rebecca gather her things. On top of her pile of birthday cards is one from "Your friends and teachers at Holy Sisters Academy." When your school relies on parent and alumnae donations, they do make the extra effort.

I open the card. "Holy . . ."

"Yeah, it's a prayer. Why so surprised?"

It's not the message ("Have a blessed birthday!") that has my jaw hanging: it's one of the signatures. A familiar, looping script. But I can't quite place a face with the name: Sister Verna.

"Rebecca, who is this?"

"I don't . . . oh, yeah. That's Sister Spacey."

Then I remember the nameplate on her desk.

The card is no longer a card.

It's Exhibit A.

I'm not thinking anything else when I start to slide it into my bag.

"Hey!" Rebecca snatches the card from my hand. "You're stealing my birthday card?"

"What?"

"Jessica, you have a problem." Of course I do! I just found out an HSA teacher is behind the threatening notes I've been getting at school! "A *kleptomaniac* problem."

Sigh.

I have so many problems, it defies probability that Rebecca has picked one that I *don't* have.

I would like to thank my makeup artist, my hairdresser, my stylist, the photographers who have been airbrushing my pictures for years, and my manicurists, who have been scraping the crust off of my elbows and feet for years. It's all an image, and if you want to be truly hot . . . be yourself.

—JESSICA ALBA

(in her acceptance speech on being named Choice Hottie at the Teen Choice Awards)

scene 1

Eva's happy humming fills the limo. The Jane Austen director agreed to audition her. He's going to choose an evening around her *Two Sisters* schedule.

Her smile is camera-ready. "All it took was a little persistence." And a willingness to lie to her mom and her agent, drop her sister in a hot, stuffy room for an hour, and crash a movie set. "I've got a good feeling about the part."

"Yeah, I'm getting goose bumps."

"I was going to say that!" says Keiko. Missing my sarcasm.

E arches an eyebrow. "What's up, Jessica?"

I'm too embarrassed to say that I think Jeremy is mad at me—along with every Year Nine girl at school, especially my friends—so I focus on the revelation that Giselle turned out to be Jeremy's former *Sweetness and Sam* costar.

"Elle Marie? What's your worry?"

Keiko nods. "Please. You've maimed bigger stars than her."

Not. Helping.

Eva squeezes my hand. "Jessica, remember, if you can't fit in, stand out."

Fortune-cookie advice? Ugh.

My sister is more than usually full of herself this morning. But it's her eco-limo, so I mumble: "Thankseva."

Keiko pulls out a pen. "Beautiful sentiment, Eva! I'm writing that down!"

So. Not. Helping.

Can I bring E back to earth? "What act are you putting together for Senior Sing-out?"

" 'Big Spender.' "

"That was your song from last year!"

Eva shrugs. "I don't have time to work up a new routine for the bragging grammies. Abuela's lucky I'm fitting her in at all."

"Eva!"

"You know what I mean. Look, the Sanchez twins? Not exactly world-class competition, are they?"

All I can think is: there are different definitions of the word *class.* Eva can be the best sister in the world, but when her ambition flares, the rest of the world gets lost in the sparks.

At my old school, the teachers had a "lounge" to gather in before classes. A dressed-up word for a conference room with a fridge, a sink, and a lingering smell of tuna salad. At HSA, each teacher has a small office of his or her own.

I hurry down the hall but can't block out the buzz about Jeremy's visit to the rink. Somehow all the cool is credited to Giselle, none to Rebecca. Or me.

"I know I'm outing myself as Someone Who's Pathetically Excited to See a Celebrity, but he's so cute!"

"Are he and Giselle dating?"

"They were each other's first kiss on *Sweetness and Sam*. . . . It's destiny."

Not what I want to hear.

I hold my hands over my ears and whistle loudly as I rush by. Sure to improve my reputation around here.

I knock at the smooth wooden door. "Sister? Hello?"

"Come in."

Sister Spacey sits in front of a heavy metal desk with, surprisingly, a laptop. Piles of books—mostly Bible studies—bury a table and two chairs; leaning towers of folders threaten to collapse; and every surface is covered with Post-its marked with looping script.

She looks up from her desk. "Yes?" I see that her blue eyes are actually quite sharp behind her wide plastic-rimmed glasses. Wisps of white hair escape the frame of her blue habit.

Suddenly, I'm not sure what to say. When I saw her signature on Rebecca's birthday card, I knew she was behind the Post-it notes with the cryptic messages. But now I wonder: were the notes really meant for me? Sister Spacey barely seems to recognize me.

I reach into my backpack and pull out the envelope that contains the two notes I found and the one Ingrid gave me. The words *danger, loss, destruction,* and *murder* jump out at me. "These are yours."

She reaches for the notes. She looks pleased, then guarded. "Thank you." She levels her first direct look at me. "Goodbye."

Even with my curiosity burning—*What are the Post-its? Notes to herself? To someone else?*—her tone pushes me to the door.

I pick up my bag.

I put it down again. I have to know: "What are the notes about?"

She considers ignoring my question. Instead, she chooses each word carefully. "I'm helping some students."

Students go to Sister Spacey for guidance? Hard to imagine. And how would talk about betrayal and murder help anyone? Is this some kind of seriously old-school therapy? Yet I look at her solemn face and believe she's telling me the truth. Especially when she adds: "It's time for you to go, isn't it?"

For someone tiny, elderly, and perpetually zoned out, she can find focus when she wants to.

I'm halfway around the corner when the first bell rings. I realize that not only am I late, but I left my backpack in Sister's office.

Her door is closed when I go back. I hear voices through the wood. The principal has joined her.

"I heard what you told that girl."

"I did not lie to her."

"It . . . almost seemed as if you were going to tell her the real truth."

Pause.

"Well, I wasn't going to."

My curiosity?

Oh, yeah, it's burning again. Hot.

scene 2

Sister Spacey was not telling me the "real" truth about her mystery notes, but the odd little nun is an unlikely suspect for rampaging through lockers, swiping photos, and composing threatening magnet messages. She didn't even notice when I reached through the door to grab my backpack.

If the notes aren't related to the locker break-ins, does that reveal anything new about who might be framing me?

I return to the scene of the crime to grab my books

before homeroom: the locker alcove. My heart jumps when I see that a green folded paper has been put (*planted?*) in my locker.

I unfold it slowly, practically squeezing into my locker so no one else can see it. The brochure is headlined: *Taking Control of Taking: Living with Kleptomania*.

Rebecca and I need to have a serious talk. Now.

Rebecca and I are supposed to be discussing our service requirement for the year—all Year Nine students have to perform ten hours of charity work—but instead I'm spilling all: how Jeremy's photo was stolen; how the locker magnets spelled out "Don't you dare"; how the thefts seemed timed for when I looked like the most obvious suspect; and, finally, the scene she witnessed: how the stolen photos were dumped in my locker.

She seems to believe me. "This started on your second day? And you didn't know anyone here?"

"Alex Banks and Ingrid are the only students I'd even seen before HSA." I hadn't seen Alex on my first day, and Ingrid didn't stand out in my mind. One person did. "But

Giselle was giving me the stink eye before we'd even spoken."

"Eureka!" Rebecca snaps her fingers. "That's Greek for I've figured it out."

Suddenly Giselle's motive is clear to me, too. "She's jealous of Eva! E is on a show with Jeremy when she's not anymore."

Rebecca frowns. "Has she ever mentioned anything about Eva? What would the locker message have to do with your sister?"

"It's got to be about Eva somehow. . . ."

Rebecca smirks. "How long have you been Eva's little sister?"

Duh. All my life. "What does that have to do with it?"

"Everything." The bell rings for us to change classes. "Meet me at the student newspaper office tomorrow before school. We'll find some proof for what I've figured out."

"Which is?"

She gives a smug smile. "Stay tuned."

Grr . . . I make a comment about her mother's smooth forehead. But that little melonfarmer? She's not talking.

Scene 3

The locker thefts can't eat at me, because, when it comes down to it, I know I didn't do anything wrong.

What I told Jeremy at the Moonlight? The lie about Leo being my cousin? Yeah, that's still nibbling.

I talk over some options with Petunia—an expert listener—and it comes down to: not being quite brave enough to call Jeremy on the phone.

I punch in a text message:

> Thx for coming
> last night! Sorry
> I was so lame at
> the rink. Leo's
> not my cousin.
> Just a friend.

If I had called Jeremy, I would have worried he could hear my heart pounding over the line.

He writes back:

```
U r a terrible
liar, Jess. Only
bad 1 I know. ;)
(PS: I only went
because u said
there were going
to be prep-school
guys there. How
lame is that?)
```

Jeremy wanted to make sure there wasn't some TMS guy I'd like more than him?

That is lame.

Very, very lame.

If *lame* is another word for "the best news I've heard all day—or any day ever in my previous almost-fourteen years."

He continues:

```
R u looking out
4 Elle?
```

Right after theology, Giselle got in my face about "blowing off" the first round of musical tryouts, saying I shouldn't think I can walk in at the last minute and steal the show.

As she swished away, Rebecca called after her, "That's just the crazy *walking*!" (Rebecca still can't believe I didn't know that Giselle was Sweetness—Giselle looks completely different, but it was just one of those facts that everyone knows. Like the walls were supposed to whisper it to me.)

So what can I tell Jeremy except:

```
Of course I'm
looking out
4 her!
```

Tomorrow I'll be doing more "looking out for Elle"—when I try to prove that she's behind Project Photo Frame-Up. And that she's messed with the wrong Ortiz sister.

```
U r the best!
```

Ugh. Jeremy's text makes me feel like the worst. The worst friend, that is.

But he doesn't know the real Giselle . . . does he?

Eva knocks on my door. She's holding her Chanel lace-up boots.

"I thought these would look better on you."

Even Petunia looks suspicious.

E has never thought any of her things that she had not outgrown and worn a hole through and watched go completely out of fashion would look better on me. She shares her clothes, but usually with warnings against spilling/sneezing/breathing on them, and sometimes with a price. To borrow her Stella McCartney trench coat, I had to take an extra bingo night with Abuela.

Uh-freaking-oh.

"Eva, what's going on?" The Senior Sing-Out is tomorrow.

"My Jane Austen audition is set for tomorrow night. At six."

"The Sing-Out starts at six."

"There's a chance I could make it." And a chance she'll

blow off our grandmother in front of all her friends. A chance Eva is willing to take. "I can't change the audition time. You know I'm lucky the director is seeing me at all."

"Did you tell Abuela? Mom and Dad?"

"It will be easier to tell them I'm not going if I can say you are."

"But—"

Eva makes the calm-down gesture with her hands. "Don't worry. You'd be in the audience as usual. That would be enough. No one would expect more."

"Hey." Hold the bar a little lower, why don't you? Of course, the idea of me performing onstage is an impossible one.

Then: my thoughts freeze.

Eva's words are the final clue in Project Photo Frame-Up. The missing motivation is suddenly . . . found.

Eva takes my split second of silence as the answer she wants. She hugs me, dropping the boots on my chair. "Thanks, Jessica. I knew I could count on you."

Behind us, Petunia heaves her heavy-breathing self off the floor to start chewing on the laces. Because Little P? She never changes.

Scene 4

Bright and early, Mom drops me off at the front gates of TMS. The newspaper office is a small white wooden building shared by the two schools.

"I'll think of something for the Sing-Out tonight, Mom. Promise."

Mom hides her frown. If she's frustrated with Eva, she doesn't want me to worry about it. "Jessica, you don't have to fix everything." She pushes a strand of hair behind my ear. "Eva's career is getting bigger. She's going to deal with that. Your dad and I are going to deal with that. You're going to school and work on this journalism project, right?"

"Right." Journalism project. Because "clue-catching for Project Photo Frame-Up" wasn't going to get Mom out of bed early this morning.

"I'm glad you're taking an interest in extracurricular activities, *m'ija*."

Mamacita, if you only knew.

Rebecca and Ally meet me at the gate, since I don't know the TMS campus. Of course we're all dressed alike—except Ally's hair is hidden under a newsboy cap.

Rebecca caught Ally up on the locker thefts, so she knows what I'm talking about when I say: "It's Giselle."

Rebecca nods. "Figured that out, huh?"

I couldn't see Giselle's motivation because I couldn't stop seeing myself as "the sister." The first thing I said at orientation—after my name—was that I'm Eva's sister! I thought I was running back to my old reputation, but it was my old *identity* as the person people thought of in terms of my older, glamorous, starry sister. And it skewed how I saw everything about Project Photo Frame-Up.

I would have figured everything out sooner except I couldn't see any way that I was a threat to Giselle. I needed a new perspective:

- **The way spelling "car" backward forced me to think about car culture in a new way**

- **The way a trip to Boston opened Mom's eyes to the *Shopping Time* ads she'd seen all her life**

- **The way being away from HSA made me step back and realize that *I* could be the target of a smear campaign**

- **The way a move to Beverly Hills changed how Leo and I deal with each other**

- **The way Eva's assuming that I could not take the stage at the Sing-Out suddenly rankled me**

That's why Rebecca could see it before me. She had a new perspective. For her—and for Giselle—it was believable that I could be an actress/singer/dancing sensation.

Ultimately, it was E's behavior that clued me in to the

way Giselle was thinking. How Eva didn't tell Paige about the improv portion of the *Malice* audition—even though it was a role E didn't want. And the lengths E went to to land the Jane Austen audition—lying to Mom about where we were going, crashing the Athenaeum set, stranding me, and, tonight, disappointing our *abuela*.

Bottom line: top actresses are competitive.

You don't wind up on a movie marquee without fighting off your rivals, any more than you wind up tennis champion, first-chair violinist, or valedictorian.

Actresses? They're just better at *acting* like it comes without a struggle.

Giselle had been a top actress, and—*Great Shades of Sharpay!*—she still has the competitive streak. Even if what she's competing for now is the lead role in school musicals and chorales.

Giselle's reason for framing me? She thought I could be the new top DQ! Fooled by rumors—and my admittedly rock-the-house poetry presentation—she was fighting back.

The timing falls into place: how Giselle wasn't at dance class for the first theft, and the threatening "DON'T YOU

DARE" message on the day the *Annie Get Your Gun* tryout list was posted. I should have been more alert all along, but I hadn't realized I was the target then.

Me.

Jessica Lucia Ortiz.

Project Photo Frame-Up has been about me from the beginning. Of course, it's a sweet-voiced, dramatic, stuffed-with-star-quality me who I will never be . . . but still! Me!

Keiko was right. I never should have let someone else determine my image.

Is everything about publicity?

In Hollywood and high school . . . yeah.

scene 5

Rebecca is Googling background information on Giselle. Ally and I are looking through old issues of the *Herald*—the HSA/TMS newspaper. We're searching for anything that can link Giselle to the thefts.

"What about this?" says Rebecca. "Giselle was in a

TV series called *Safecrackers.* All about breaking and entering."

Hmm . . . it's something. You'd hardly need to have worked with burglary experts to bust open a locker, but it's a link. I think about all the training that Jeremy has been going through—before *Space Frontier: The Movie* films, he really will be able to kickbox and fence. Maybe Giselle had real-world preparation for *Safecrackers,* too?

Outside, we can hear the boys on the TMS water polo team practicing. If pushing each other off the diving board and holding inner tubes for each other to jump through counts. I think they're doing wind sprints every ten minutes, but then I realize that they all jump out of the pool whenever a sightseeing tour bus goes by. To make rude gestures.

"Ten laps!" shouts their coach when they splash back in. A price they're happy to pay.

At least one guy isn't in the pool. Will Dorsey rolls into the room.

He looks surprised to see us. "The first newspaper meeting isn't till next week."

"It's another kind of investigation." Rebecca explains

all as he wheels to a large desk. It looks like Will has been very involved with the newspaper by the way he's pulling supplies out of the desk. The poster above the desk reads:

SUNDAY MONDAY TUESDAY WEDNESDAY THURSDAY FRIDAY SATURDAY
THERE IS NO SOMEDAY.

That seems Will-like, too. He's not letting anyone else decide his image.

Will rolls over to Ally. Her cap is pulled tight against her head—it's hard to believe that mountain of red hair can fit under there. Ally is the opposite of a good detective. She keeps getting distracted by the articles and pictures instead of looking for clues. "I like what you said in your op-ed last year, Will. 'War is a failure of the imagination.'"

"That's from an Alan Moore graphic novel. Good stuff."

Another reason Ally is a bad detective? She doesn't believe anybody would set out to frame a person. Only that two people might fail to fully understand each other's point of view. Can she really slap all the world's problems with a big "*oops*" Band-Aid?

Rebecca comes to my side. Her voice is low. "Ally is pretty, right? The friendly thing? Plus all that hair."

I whisper back. "Rebecca? Are all those fencing dates just a distraction from Will?"

"Will locked me in the friend box." Rebecca does the mime thing, pushing her hands against invisible walls. "Hopeless."

"I thought you only liked guys with hidden deviant behavior."

"He's a three-time junior Scrabble champion."

Oh. That *is* deviant.

"Our parents worked together last summer, and I tried all the magazine article catch-your-crush stuff—unnecessary touching, getting interested in his interests. My sudden passion for the Paralympics? Hard to play that casually."

"And you chose the roller rink for your birthday—?"

" 'Cause he might come." Rebecca groans. "Man, look at him."

He is supercute. Even with that scratchy-looking goatee.

"You might have a chance."

Rebecca sighs. "Please, he's so ten minutes away."

I glance down at the old *Herald* in my lap. It has a photo

of Will from last year—he was named Year Eight spelling champion. With no goatee. He wasn't Peach Fuzz then.

My brain buzzes.

I wave the paper, getting Ally's and Will's attention. "Giselle called Will Peach Fuzz in English class. But she wouldn't have seen him with the goatee yet if she hadn't been spying on our ballroom dancing—when she said she was on the other side of campus."

"Only she wasn't, because she was stealing from Ingrid's locker!" Rebecca claps.

But I'm not celebrating yet. "How can we prove it?"

Will looks thoughtful. "It could be a good story for the newspaper."

He's in.

Ally bends over to look at my *Herald*. Her cap tumbles off.

And then it's all over except for the shouting.

Scene 6

"Hey, Peach Fuzz! I'm ready for my close-up."

After school, in the back of the HSA library, Rebecca and I are tucked behind a bookcase. Will is at a nearby table with his *Herald* tape recorder and notepad. Giselle arrives to talk about the upcoming school musical.

Or so she thinks.

Will starts off throwing softballs. "What do you think of this year's choice of musical?"

"I'm going to rock that solo—"You Can't Get a Man with a Gun."

"So the roles have been cast?"

"No. Not officially."

Crouched beside me, Rebecca is showing some poor detective instincts. She's not focused on the moment. She's still disappointed with Ally. "She grows it out for eight years. One comment from Dax—and *chop-chop*."

"She didn't say it was for him."

"Did she have to? You didn't know her before, Jessica.

She was really independent and fun—now she doesn't know what she thinks till Dax tells it to her. She should be with us, but she said he needed help with a quiz tomorrow. A *quiz*!"

Or Ally might have been tired of Rebecca's horror reaction to her new look. Ally's miles of strawberry-blond curls? Chopped, cut, gone. And without the weight to pull it down, her shorter hair is coiled close to her head. It's a big change.

And speaking of a big change . . . this behind-the-scenes sister is about to take the stage. "Let's go."

I step around the bookcase and come up beside Giselle.

Rebecca is at my side. She shouts, "Yippee-kai-yay, melonfarmers!"

Why does she shout that?

No. Freaking. Idea.

Giselle and Will turn to stare at Rebecca. Then at me. I take a deep breath. "Giselle, I know you've been setting me up as the photo thief." Giselle gives Will a confused look. But I keep going. "Do I have to *spell* it out for you?"

I lay out all the pieces of Project Photo Frame-Up: the timing, the evidence planted against me, the motivation, the way she called Will Peach Fuzz when supposedly she hadn't seen him since last year.

Giselle stares me down. "I see a lot of accusations, and no proof."

Well.

Yes.

Noticed that, did she?

I was hoping the need to confess might overwhelm her. Sadly, she and I have not been reading the same mystery novels.

I glance at Will. He's the extra element. He clears his throat. "Sounds like something the *Herald* should look into."

Giselle narrows her eyes at me. She is not going to crack. But would she take an out if I offered her one? When it comes down to it, war *is* a failure of the imagination. I don't want a battle with Giselle—she's both a tough enemy and a friend of Jeremy's. Would she trade a favor she needs badly for one that I need? Just as badly.

Let's find out.

Scene 7

"Worst. Plan. Ever."

Giselle and I are in the back of my dad's Nissan, whispering so that my parents can't hear us from the front seat. I could tell Giselle that actually I've had way worse plans than this one—plans that have resulted in some freaky jinx consequences—but I don't think that would make her feel better.

It sure doesn't make *me* feel better.

But sniping back at Giselle might. "Look who's talking. The girl who doesn't even find out if the competition *is* competition before she attacks."

"Enough, Ortiz." Then: "You can't sing? At all?" That was almost the hardest part of the whole plan—convincing Giselle that I needed her. She still thinks it's a trap.

"Listen, I'll sing the school song. That will convince you." I open my mouth. "H—"

"Stop."

"But I'm going to convince you."

"You did. That was awful."

The first note—the first letter—of the song did it. I try to congratulate myself on being so convincing.

Yay, me.

Giselle sighs deeply. Her mind is on better days. "I wore Swarovski crystal–studded heels to the Golden Globes when I was eight years old, and now this. . . ."

Yeah, yeah, the karma fairy is kicking your butt. Welcome to my life.

Mom looks back at us. "All set, girls?"

Giselle nods seriously. She's playing the part of my new best friend. "Oh, yes, Mrs. Ortiz. I'm so looking forward to this evening with the St. Joseph's Bingo League."

Mom beams.

The girl can act.

Phew.

☆

The plan—worst ever or not—is that I'll go up onstage and lip-synch the words that Giselle sings from behind the curtain. She's been perfecting her rendition of "You Can't Get a Man with a Gun" for the school play. As we drive along, I keep my printout of the lyrics in front of me, perfecting *my* rendition—moving my lips to the music.

My conscience squawks that this has the making of a Senior Sing-Out scandal—but I can't let my *abuela* down. Not in front of all her friends.

Of course, I've never had to open my mouth onstage before, but I have a plan. When the spotlight comes on, I'm going to . . . *one-two-three* . . . float out of my body! Exactly like I did for the poetry class!

I'd feel better if I remembered how I had done that—or if I had planned to do it in the first place—but I'm working with what I have: an absent sister, a bragging *abuela,* a penchant for shy spasms, a mom and dad in the audience, and a jealous rival turned (I hope!) ally.

We push open the doors to the St. Joseph's auditorium, and there's the crowd, there's the stage, but where's the curtain?

There's no curtain!

Nothing for Giselle to hide behind!

Right about now would be a good time to practice that leaving-my-body (and my problems) trick.

scene 8

"Abuela! Abuela! Where's the curtain?"

My *abuela* is done up in more than her usual finery. Dangling gold earrings in the shape of songbirds, a flowing purple pantsuit, and ropes of shiny necklaces.

"Jessica, *mi bonita*!" Abuela hugs me, then Mom and Dad. She shakes hands with Giselle. She won't let me say a word until she has had her moment of greeting and of pointing out the new décor of the auditorium: the tables have been rolled away, thin blue cushions cover the rows of foldout chairs, and shiny paper stars are taped to the walls.

Oooh-Freaking-Aaah.

Now, where's that curtain?

"*Cálmate, niña*. The curtain is out for cleaning. I know why you are worried."

"You do?"

She nods. "Stage fright."

You.

Have.

No.

Idea.

"Abuela, listen, please—"

Her hearing problem takes over. If there's a problem, Abuela does not want to hear it. "Jessica, it meant so much when you called to say that you would take Eva's place."

"Abuela, *por favor . . .*"

"But you cannot take her place. Do you know why?"

Because E is a multitalented professional actress and I'm a vocally challenged walking bad-luck case?

"Because, *mi amor,* you have your own place. Your talent—that's what we celebrate tonight. *¿Entiendes?* "

Mom and Dad are smiling hugely. But what do they know about reality? They love me.

Only Giselle gets it. One skeptical eyebrow is raised. High.

The world does not have enough shy people. The problems of the planet are largely caused by outgoing people—like all the people out going, "Hey, listen up: your country? I want it."

We shy folks never look for trouble. Once people realize this, it will become cool to be shy. They'll notice me hiding out at parties behind the chip bowl, and quietly approach. "You're amazing. How did you get so . . . shy?"

I will only smile and say nothing.

Until that blissful day, I am sweating it out in the front row of the Senior Sing-Out with my family. We sit through the cute acts (toddlers showboating or forgetting lines) and the longest-five-minutes-on-earth acts (elementary school kids' flutophone recitals). Every time I want to freak out about my debut, Abuela reaches over and pats my hand.

What can I say to her? What can I do? I've been going to Catholic school for weeks, but it's the Senior Sing-Out that has me praying hard. For a miracle.

When the Sanchez twins take the stage, they give their best performance ever. Out with last year's not-so-dramatic reading from *Little Women*, and in with tap-dancing and baton twirling.

Make that *flaming* baton twirling. *Whoa!*

Plus they've got an extra spark that's from more than just lighter fluid. Maybe it's the professional coaching. Or maybe it's knowing that the wrong Ortiz sister is taking the stage next.

Mrs. Sanchez is still glowing from the twins' performance when she picks up the microphone. That's why she sounds a little cocky (for a white-haired eighty-year-old who has a heavy hand with the blue eye shadow): "And now, please welcome Jessica Ortiz. Granddaughter of Lucia Ortiz."

"Come, *bonita*." Abuela takes my hand and pulls me to the stage. I'm desperately trying to remember exactly *why* you can't get a man with a gun when Abuela takes the microphone. "This is my Jessica. She has a lovely talent. Every Christmas and birthday card from when she was a small girl I have saved because of her way with words."

The old upright piano is pushed onto the stage. Abuela sits in front of it. "For tonight, I set her words to music for all of us to enjoy. This is from a card she dictated to her mother for me when she was a little girl." She pats the bench for me to sit beside her.

What card? What is Abuela talking about? My fingers tighten on the crushed *Annie Get Your Gun* lyrics in my hand.

Abuela removes a folded card from her pocket. The

creases are worn. There is a crayon drawing of a man's face with a gray mustache. The card opens to reveal Mom's neat handwriting.

Abuela's fingers touch the keys. Her strong alto fills the air.

"Abuela, Abuela,
I'm thinking of you.
Abuela, Abuela,
Don't be sad.

"Daddy told me Papa Aldo
Went to heaven.
He should look for
My friend's dog, Thor.
A brown-spotted dog.
He runs after cars.
But not anymore.

"Abuela, Abuela,
I'm thinking of you.
I like that your house

Smells like a Christmas store.
I like that when Daddy
says not to spoil me,
You do it some more.

"Abuela, Abuela,
I'm thinking of you.
Papa Aldo didn't talk so much—
Because snoring does not count.
But he had talking eyes. That is true.
Happy, talking eyes
when he looked at you."

Abuela's fingers slip on the keys, but suddenly Giselle is there beside her. They sing the song together. I have to give Giselle credit—she was just as surprised as I was by Abuela's taking the stage, but her innate theatricality takes over . . . and her incredible soprano brings real sweetness to the words.

Abuela and Giselle finish the last line in harmony: " 'Happy, talking eyes when he looked at you.' "

The audience is applauding, especially Mom and Dad. There's no official winner of the Senior Sing-Out.

But unofficially?

It's a night I won't ever forget.

Scene 9

The St. Joseph's auditorium is rocking. Big-band music is playing on the stereo. The hugs and kisses are piling up for me and Giselle and Abuela. Mr. Singh is shouting "Bingo!" every few minutes. It's so festive, I suspect someone has slipped real sugar into those glucose-free muffins.

Eva rushes in from the back of the room and heads right for me. "Those Sanchez twins must have rocked. I could hear the cheers from the parking lot." She is pulling on the shiny black top hat of her "Big Spender" costume. "Don't worry, Abuela. I'm here."

Abuela takes E's arm. "Thank you for coming, *mi amor*. Sit down. Have a muffin."

Even as Abuela leads her away, E isn't quite getting it. As we say in bingoland, she should have gotten here "B-4," not after.

Giselle nods at me. She's ready to go. "My dad's here."

"Thanks, Giselle. You were great. Your voice . . . big wow." I reach for my backpack. I pull out a package.

She puts her hands up. "You didn't have to get me anything."

Yes, I did.

The package is full of the HSA photos that need to be returned. A major mystery is left: how is Giselle going to explain the thefts at school?

I'll be watching her.

I don't think I could tear my eyes away.

After Giselle leaves, Mom corners me at the stereo. As I suspected: nothing recorded in the last fifty years is available.

Pride and smugness are battling on Mom's face. "You're feeling better?"

I nod.

"And it's not because of a boy?" Mom shamelessly reminds me of her Boston pep talk about a cute boyfriend not solving all problems.

I nod again.

She resists saying, "I told you so."

All through the rest of the party.

All through the drive home.

All through the walk from the car to the front door.

Right up until she's turning the key in the lock. "Told. You. So."

scene 10

Giselle is cast as the lead. Not in *Annie Get Your Gun*. That's not official yet. She's the star of Project Photo Rescue.

". . . and as I held his hand and walked him to the halfway house, I managed to slip the photos into my backpack."

Giselle wipes at her tear-slicked cheeks. The Year Nine girls are gathered around her and the pile of "rescued" photos on the Great Lawn. Giselle went completely urban legend with a story about a young janitor's assistant here at HSA. Haunted by his tragic past, he sometimes was not strong enough to fight his locker-theft impulses. Giselle confronted him, rescued the photos, and helped him get the counseling he needed. The plot sounds loosely based on an episode from her *Safecrackers* TV show.

Basic-cable slumming? Indeed.

If I had met this janitor's assistant and this situation *truly* had happened to me, no one would believe it.

The way Giselle tells it? The DQs and Scholars are swallowing it down like milk with cereal. *Gulp-gulpety-gulp.*

"Thanks for returning my Mathletes photo." Keneesha hands Giselle a tissue. "I owe you."

Giselle can turn on the tears. I'm impressed until I notice something peeking from the side pocket of her bag. Is it a white lipstick in a clear case? I breathe deep and catch a whiff of menthol. Yep: a tear stick.

Rebecca grabs up her Baffles photo. She whispers to

me: "No one is even questioning why we never saw this guy around."

"She explained that he 'kept to the shadows.' " I think she stole that one from a Tempest Hott novel. "And besides, she's *good*."

I don't see Ally around, so I slip her pictures of Dax into my bag.

Then I spot it. There, at the bottom of the pile. My photo of Jeremy. I grab for it and feel Giselle's eyes on me.

I look up and just miss the expression on her face.

A wink? A smirk?

Time will tell.

Scene 11

Did you ever buy something—red Converse sneakers, great-fitting new jeans, a get-well card for Reese Witherspoon—and then notice that everyone around you seemed to have just bought the same thing?

Maybe not so much with the get-well card.

But sometimes I wonder, are there suddenly more red Converse sneakers than ever before? Or is it that I'm clued into them now?

Same with cryptic little Post-it notes. This one is crumpled up beside the garbage can in Spanish class. Sister Spacey monitors a study hall in this room right before we come in.

No one else seems to notice, but I can't get my eyes off the paper. My fingers close around it before the first person is even out the door for lunch.

I read the new mysterious warning. And then I notice what first looks like a spelling error.

And then looks like a clue.

Can you guess what the misspelled word is? Are you getting warmer? And what comes after warm . . . ?

A trip to the library might reveal the real truth behind Sister Spacey's secret notes.

☆

I go straight to the mystery section. It's fully stocked with Raven O'Rourke books. I flip to the back covers for the story summaries.

Yep. I knew those plots sounded familiar.

Hott Water is a version of the Noah story, with Tempest captaining a cruise ship instead of an ark; *Hott Fashion* is taken from Joseph and his coat of many colors; *Hott Sand,* the story of Moses; and *Hott Summer,* Jonah and the whale.

Each story is based on the Bible. I put that clue together with the last note:

Jealousy clouds
thinking—
drives rival into
harm's way
Hott Danger

At first I had thought the word *Hott* was misspelled—but not if it's the title of the next Tempest Hott book. . . . Perhaps a version of the story of David—who sent Bathsheba's husband into battle to have her all to himself.

Could Sister Spacey *be* thriller writer Raven O'Rourke? Looking closer, I see that *Raven* unravels into *Verna*! Sister's real name!

It's Verna/Raven/Spacey's notes for future books that are littering the halls. While zoned out in study hall, is she mentally commanding zoo animals, two by two, aboard a rescue ship?

She said she was "helping students." She didn't lie—technically. Her book profits pay for scholarships—but she did misdirect. Like how I was going to take the stage but have Giselle behind the curtain. "Raven" is onstage while the tiny elderly nun is behind the curtain. Even I assumed that the author had to be a former DQ type. Wrong!

I guess it wouldn't help Raven's image—or book sales—if the truth was known.

Star quality is hiding in some unlikely places here in L.A.

Or is that true everywhere?

Scene 12

A squashed sneeze?

Asthma problem?

No, it's . . . the sound of someone trying not to cry. I didn't recognize the noise because it's so mismatched to where I am. The plush carpet and neat rows of books feel out of order with big emotion.

I put down *Hott Water*—the story kind of sucked me in—and peer around the shelves. There, in the exact quiet spot where I hid out after finding the stolen photos, is Ally.

Her head is bent, her cropped curls resting on her arms. She looks up at me. "Oh. Hey, Jessica."

Her eyes are tragic, and I get a bad feeling.

The boyfriend! He made her cut her hair and now he's dumped her! That melonfarmer!

"Do you want to talk?" 'Cause I'll jump on a boy-bashing bandwagon if needed. Angry teen chicks unite!

Ally gulps hard. "I m-miss m-my hair!"

Oh.

Not dumped, just shorn.

Maybe I shouldn't expect to ace the psychology part of World Cultures. "It's a big change, Ally. You're getting used to it."

"You don't understand." She hangs her head. "I'm being so s-superficial."

Then she explains. And I realize that I underestimated Ally, even though the evidence about what kind of person she is was there from the first day—the way she welcomed me, her Web page motto, the poem she chose, how she believes the best about people.

☆

It's the first official meeting of the *Herald*—the school newspaper being one of the activities that HSA and TMS run together. Twelve of us from Year Six to Year Twelve squeeze into the small newspaper office. A short, chubby Year Twelve guy with dark-rimmed glasses hands out sign-up sheets.

Will, Rebecca, and I are the only Year Nine students. I have a story to tell. Will has an interest in journalism. Rebecca has an interest in Will.

The newspaper editor gives us the drill: we'll meet to pitch ideas on Mondays after school, with finished articles due on Thursdays.

The editor looks surprised when the meeting breaks up and I leave my article with him. "We haven't assigned anything yet."

"The story came to me." It didn't wait to be called.

Star Quality

What is star quality? Coming to HSA got me thinking about that—probably because star quality is paying my tuition.

Is it the way that some girls turn heads when they walk on a stage? Is it the way that an amazing soprano can take ordinary words and make them (you know it's coming) sing?

That's the talent-show

part of star quality. The people who have gifts and share them in a big way. But there is talent that isn't showy.

Ally McNamara, Year Nine, cut off her hair. No, I'm not going to write about her talent for personal styling. She saw a TV show about Locks of Love—the charity that takes donated hair of ten inches or longer and creates wigs for children who have long-term medical hair loss. She was inspired.

Now Ally's new look doesn't fit the mold for a typical star on a typical magazine cover. We know those photos are airbrushed, and that the actresses have hair extensions, plus professional makeup and wardrobe help. But it can be hard to challenge all the images that come at us. So my new definition is that it's star quality when it opens my eyes to the possibilities—and the person—I hadn't really seen before.

Ally almost didn't recognize the girl in her own mirror. She had to ask me, did she look all right?

I told her the truth: she looked like a star.

scene 13

A ringtone. Can you guess why it would fill me with unreasonable happiness? Two clues:

- **Jeremy Jones's cell**
- **Van Morrison's "Brown-Eyed Girl"**

Now, maybe Jeremy just has a thing for Irish folk-rockers, but I'd like to think he's not totally opposed to brown-eyed girls. Or else why would he be on a dream date with this one?

That's right: the *Sound of Music* sing-along at the Hollywood Bowl! Our seats face the huge screen set up in the band shell. The movie will run with all the lyrics shown at the bottom of the screen.

Plus my parents are fully five rows away!

I would complain that they are crashing my date except that I'm crashing theirs. They found out about extra tickets right when Jeremy was texting me.

Jeremy looks a bit surprised by the preshow costume contest and parade. There are whole families dressed up as "My Favorite Things" (from "warm woolen mittens" to "whiskers on kittens"), little girls who look like nuns—one eerily like Sister Spacey—and of course the place is lousy with lederhosen.

I can't wait another minute to open the free props bag. I know that Jeremy is used to scoring thousands of dollars of bling-and-things at the swag suites of awards shows, but can his free Xboxes, plane tickets, and spa passes compete with this treasure trove?

- **Song cards with question marks, pieces of drapery, and plastic edelweiss—each for waving during the appropriate songs**
- **An invitation to the ball given by Captain von Trapp and the fiancée he'll soon be dropping like a hot plate**

 **A plastic popper for use during the First Kiss (turn the bottom to pop out the confetti)**

Jeremy raises an eyebrow—overwhelmed by the magic of it all. Possibly.

Could this evening be more special? Only because it's Jeremy's only free one in weeks. And this is how he's spending it.

"Any nuns like Maria at your school?"

"No singing, dancing Nazi resisters." But definitely one who isn't as she first appears. "What's your favorite part in the movie?"

He shrugs. "Don't have one. You?"

"The dance. When it's finally obvious that the captain likes Maria."

"Finally? You can see it in the first frame of the first shot."

"No way. There was nothing there."

"Not much for clues, are you?" Jeremy grins. "Jessica, you do know that *I* like you? Right? A lot."

THE HOLLYWOOD HILLS ARE ALIVE

WITH THE SOUND OF MUSIC!

Words fail me.

The big, goofy grin—unfortunately—does not.

Jeremy continues. "I asked if you were a model in our first conversation."

Okay, with a librarian mom, I cannot resist the fact-check. "You mean when you were accusing me of sabotaging the set? And then asked if I was a hand model? Or elbow model."

Jeremy looks surprised. "Great memory you've got there, Jess. Good to know." He pauses. "Good. To. Know." He takes my hand, which immediately becomes the focal point of all feeling in my body. Explain that, science class. "Thanks for giving Elle another chance. The way you handled it . . . it was so Jessica."

Eva spilled some of the details on Project Photo Frame-Up—how Giselle chose to serve her time at the Senior Sing-Out instead of in the hallways of HSA.

So Jessica. I always thought if my name was ever turned

into an adjective, it would have some definition like "jinxed" or "unlucky," or "why is that on fire?" But Jeremy says it like he can't think of a better way to describe something.

I smile at him. He smiles back.

Thank God he likes completely inarticulate girls!

On-screen, Julie Andrews starts twirling on that mountainside. And moments later, Jeremy is fast asleep. The first thing I think is: oh no! He's going to miss the "Edelweiss" finale, when we all wave our open cell phones and create a field of blue and white flickering lights. The next thing I think is: rest is the best thing for his sore throat. And for his eardrums—I can't stop myself from joining in once that "Do-Re-Mi" song gets going.

I look around. There's no one to notice us. With a group of larger, older ladies in tight low-cut tops that proclaim *THESE* HILLS ARE ALIVE seated next to us—even a TV star can roll under the radar.

There's no one to impress.

Jeremy only came to make me happy.

And as he gently snores through "Maria," all I can think is: he did.

EXTERIOR SHOT: UNDER A DOME OF STARS, FACES ARE UPTURNED TOWARD A LARGE SCREEN. ACROSS THE FIELD, WHITE SONG CARDS LIFT LIKE WINGS.

FADE TO BLACK.

Here are three clues to where author Mary Wilcox lives: *Legally Blonde* was filmed there. *Sabrina, the Teenage Witch* was set there. Celebrities Uma Thurman, Matt Damon, and Paul Revere were born there. ;)

Visit www.hollywoodsisters.com for more information.

PSST! DON'T MISS THE NEXT BOOK IN THE *Hollywood Sisters* SERIES

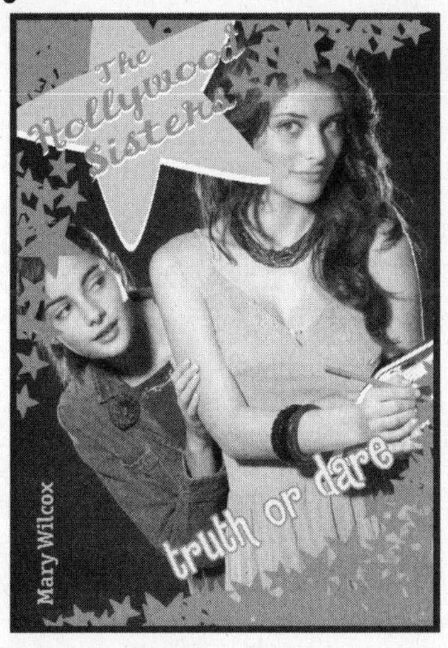

Stars. Sets. Ghosts?

Only in L.A. would a school internship involve celebrity guest stars and hitting your mark. Acting is not my thing (can you say shy spasm?) . . . but mysteries are. I'm working as an extra on my sister's latest movie, and legend has it that the mansion we're filming in is haunted. With disappearing paintings, a glowing ghost, and Eva acting possessed (by love?), I'm starting to believe the stories are true!

Chills. Thrills. Things that go bump in the night. Is my jinx on overdrive or have I stepped into a real-life horror flick?